Miss O[...]
Find[...]
Herself

BY

RADCLYFFE HALL

British Library Cataloguing-in-Publication Data
A catalogue record for this book is available from
the British Library

Radclyffe Hall

Marguerite Radclyffe Hall was born on 12th August 1880, in Bournemouth, England. Her parents separated when she was a baby and Hall was raised in a neglectful household with her mother and stepfather. She received her education at King's College London before moving to Germany to further her studies.

Hall's first novel *The Unlit Lamp* (1924) was a lengthy and grim tale that proved hard to sell. It was only published following the success of the much lighter social comedy *The Forge* (1924), which made the best-seller list of John O'London's Weekly. During the next two years she produced *A Saturday Life* (1925) and *Adam's Breed* (1926). The latter is a tale of a disenchanted head-waiter who decides to live as a hermit in a forest.. This work was well received and won both the Prix Femina Award and the James Tait Black Prize, a feat previously achieved only by E. M.

Forster's *A Passage to India* (1924).

Hall was a lesbian and had many lovers throughout her life. In 1907, she began a relationship with Mabel Batten, a well-known singer of lieder in Germany and twenty-four years her senior. Following the death of Batten's husband, the two of them moved in together and cohabited until Batten's death in 1916. The previous year, Hall had fallen for Batten's cousin Una Troubridge, a sculptor and wife of Vice-Admiral Ernest Troubridge. In 1917, Hall and Troubridge moved in together and remained a couple until Hall's death from colon cancer in 1943. Although the relationship spanned over twenty years, Hall was not a faithful partner and had many affairs of which Troubridge was painfully tolerant.

Hall is a key figure in lesbian literature for her novel *The Well of Loneliness* (1928). This is her only work with overt lesbian themes and tells the story of the life of a masculine lesbian named Stephen Gordon. This caused great controversy and was subject to an obscenity trial in Great Britain that resulted in an order for all copies to be destroyed. In the USA it was published only after a protracted legal battle. *The Well of Loneliness* ranked number seven on a list of the top 100 lesbian and gay novels compiled by The Publishing Triangle in 1999.

DEDICATED TO
OUR THREE SELVES

*All the characters represented in this book
are purely imaginary.*

AUTHOR'S FORENOTE

THIS story, which is now being published for the first time, and in which I have permitted myself a brief excursion into the realms of the fantastic, was written in July 1926, shortly before I definitely decided to write my serious study of congenital sexual inversion, *The Well of Loneliness*.

Although Miss Ogilvy is a very different person from Stephen Gordon, yet those who have read *The Well of Loneliness* will find in the earlier part of this story the nucleus of those sections of my novel which deal with Stephen Gordon's childhood and girlhood, and with the noble and selfless work done by hundreds of sexually inverted women during the Great War.

MISS OGILVY FINDS HERSELF

MISS OGILVY stood on the quay at
Calais and surveyed the disbanding of her Unit,
the Unit that together with the coming of war had
completely altered the complexion of her life, at
all events for three years.

Miss Ogilvy's thin, pale lips were set sternly and
her forehead was puckered in an effort of attention,
in an effort to memorise every small detail of every
old war-weary battered motor on whose side still
appeared the merciful emblem that had set Miss
Ogilvy free.

Miss Ogilvy's mind was jerking a little, trying
to regain its accustomed balance, trying to readjust
itself quickly to this sudden and paralysing change.
Her tall, awkward body with its queer look of
strength, its broad, flat bosom and thick legs and
ankles, as though in response to her jerking mind,
moved uneasily, rocking backwards and forwards.
She had this trick of rocking on her feet in moments
of controlled agitation. As usual, her hands were
thrust deep into her pockets, they seldom seemed
to come out of her pockets unless it were to light

a cigarette, and as though she were still standing firm under fire while the wounded were placed in her ambulances, she suddenly straddled her legs very slightly and lifted her head and listened. She was standing firm under fire at that moment, the fire of a desperate regret.

Some girls came towards her, young, tired-looking creatures whose eyes were too bright from long strain and excitement. They had all been members of that glorious Unit, and they still wore the queer little forage-caps and the short, clumsy tunics of the French Militaire. They still slouched in walking and smoked Caporals in emulation of the Poilus. Like their founder and leader these girls were all English, but like her they had chosen to serve England's ally, fearlessly thrusting right up to the trenches in search of the wounded and dying. They had seen some fine things in the course of three years, not the least fine of which was the cold, hard-faced woman who commanding, domineering, even hectoring at times, had yet been possessed of so dauntless a courage and of so insistent a vitality that it vitalised the whole Unit.

"It's rotten!" Miss Ogilvy heard someone saying. "It's rotten, this breaking up of our Unit!" And the high, rather childish voice of the speaker sounded perilously near to tears.

4

Miss Ogilvy looked at the girl almost gently, and it seemed, for a moment, as though some deep feeling were about to find expression in words. But Miss Ogilvy's feelings had been held in abeyance so long that they seldom dared become vocal, so she merely said "Oh?" on a rising inflection— her method of checking emotion.

They were swinging the ambulance cars in mid-air, those of them that were destined to go back to England, swinging them up like sacks of potatoes, then lowering them with much clanging of chains to the deck of the waiting steamer. The porters were shoving and shouting and quarrelling, pausing now and again to make meaningless gestures; while a pompous official was becoming quite angry as he pointed at Miss Ogilvy's own special car—it annoyed him, it was bulky and difficult to move.

"Bon Dieu! Mais dépêchez-vous donc!" he bawled, as though he were bullying the motor.

Then Miss Ogilvy's heart gave a sudden, thick thud to see this undignified, pitiful ending; and she turned and patted the gallant old car as though she were patting a well-beloved horse, as though she would say: "Yes, I know how it feels—never mind, we'll go down together."

Miss Ogilvy sat in the railway carriage on her way from Dover to London. The soft English landscape sped smoothly past: small homesteads, small churches, small pastures, small lanes with small hedges; all small like England itself, all small like Miss Ogilvy's future. And sitting there still arrayed in her tunic, with her forage-cap resting on her knees, she was conscious of a sense of complete frustration; thinking less of those glorious years at the Front and of all that had gone to the making of her, than of all that had gone to the marring of her from the days of her earliest childhood.

She saw herself as a queer little girl, aggressive and awkward because of her shyness; a queer little girl who loathed sisters and dolls, preferring the stable-boys as companions, preferring to play with footballs and tops, and occasional catapults. She saw herself climbing the tallest beech trees, arrayed in old breeches illicitly come by. She remembered insisting with tears and some temper that her real name was William and not Wilhelmina. All these childish pretences and illusions she remembered, and the bitterness that came after. For Miss Ogilvy

had found as her life went on that in this world it
is better to be one with the herd, that the world
has no wish to understand those who cannot con-
form to its stereotyped pattern. True enough in
her youth she had gloried in her strength, lifting
weights, swinging clubs and developing muscles,
but presently this had grown irksome to her; it
had seemed to lead nowhere, she being a woman,
and then as her mother had often protested:
muscles looked so appalling in evening dress—
a young girl ought not to have muscles.

Miss Ogilvy's relation to the opposite sex was
unusual and at that time added much to her
worries, for no less than three men had wished to
propose, to the genuine amazement of the world
and her mother. Miss Ogilvy's instinct made her
like and trust men for whom she had a pronounced
fellow-feeling; she would always have chosen them
as her friends and companions in preference to
girls or women; she would dearly have loved to
share in their sports, their business, their ideals and
their wide-flung interests. But men had not wanted
her, except the three who had found in her strange-
ness a definite attraction, and those would-be
suitors she had actually feared, regarding them
with aversion. Towards young girls and women
she was shy and respectful, apologetic and some-

7

times admiring. But their fads and their foibles, none of which she could share, while amusing her very often in secret, set her outside the sphere of their intimate lives, so that in the end she must blaze a lone trail through the difficulties of her nature.

"I can't understand you," her mother had said, "you're a very odd creature—now when I was your age . . ."

And her daughter had nodded, feeling sympathetic. There were two younger girls who also gave trouble, though in their case the trouble was fighting for husbands who were scarce enough even in those days. It was finally decided, at Miss Ogilvy's request, to allow her to leave the field clear for her sisters. She would remain in the country with her father when the others went up for the Season.

Followed long, uneventful years spent in sport, while Sarah and Fanny toiled, sweated and gambled in the matrimonial market. Neither ever succeeded in netting a husband, and when the Squire died leaving very little money, Miss Ogilvy found to her great surprise that they looked upon her as a brother. They had so often jibed at her in the past, that at first she could scarcely believe her senses, but before very long it became all too real: she it was who must straighten out endless muddles, who must make the dreary arrangements for the move, who must find a cheap but genteel house in London and, once there, who must cope with the family accounts which she only, it seemed, could balance.

It would be: "You might see to that, Wilhelmina; you write, you've got such a good head for business." Or: "I wish you'd go down and explain to that man that we really can't pay his account till next quarter." Or: "This money for the grocer is five shillings short. Do run over my sum, Wilhelmina."

Her mother, grown feeble, discovered in this daughter a staff upon which she could lean with safety. Miss Ogilvy genuinely loved her mother, and was therefore quite prepared to be leaned on; but when Sarah and Fanny began to lean too with the full weight of endless neurotic symptoms incubated in resentful virginity, Miss Ogilvy found herself staggering a little. For Sarah and Fanny were grown hard to bear, with their mania for telling their symptoms to doctors, with their unstable nerves and their acrid tongues and the secret dislike they now felt for their mother. Indeed, when old Mrs. Ogilvy died, she was unmourned except by her eldest daughter who actually felt a void in her life—the unforeseen void

9   B

that the ailing and weak will not infrequently leave behind them.

At about this time an aunt also died, bequeathing her fortune to her niece Wilhelmina who, however, was too weary to gird up her loins and set forth in search of exciting adventure—all she did was to move her protesting sisters to a little estate she had purchased in Surrey. This experiment was only a partial success, for Miss Ogilvy failed to make friends of her neighbours; thus at fifty-five she had grown rather dour, as is often the way with shy, lonely people.

When the war came she had just begun settling down—people do settle down in their fifty-sixth year—she was feeling quite glad that her hair was grey, that the garden took up so much of her time, that, in fact, the beat of her blood was slowing. But all this was changed when war was declared; on that day Miss Ogilvy's pulses throbbed wildly.

"My God! If only I were a man!" she burst out, as she glared at Sarah and Fanny, "if only I had been born a man!" Something in her was feeling deeply defrauded.

Sarah and Fanny were soon knitting socks and mittens and mufflers and Jaeger trench-helmets. Other ladies were busily working at depots, making swabs at the Squire's, or splints at the

Parson's; but Miss Ogilvy scowled and did none of these things—she was not at all like other ladies.

For nearly twelve months she worried officials with a view to getting a job out in France—not in their way but in hers, and that was the trouble. She wished to go up to the front-line trenches, she wished to be actually under fire, she informed the harassed officials.

To all her enquiries she received the same answer: "We regret that we cannot accept your offer." But once thoroughly roused she was hard to subdue, for her shyness had left her as though by magic.

Sarah and Fanny shrugged angular shoulders: "There's plenty of work here at home," they remarked, "though of course it's not quite so melodramatic!"

"Oh . . .?" queried their sister on a rising note of impatience—and she promptly cut off her hair: "That'll jar them!" she thought with satisfaction.

Then she went up to London, formed her admirable unit and finally got it accepted by the French, despite renewed opposition.

In London she had found herself quite at her ease, for many another of her kind was in London doing excellent work for the nation. It was really surprising how many cropped heads had suddenly appeared as it were out of space; how many Miss Ogilvies, losing their shyness, had come forward asserting their right to serve, asserting their claim to attention.

There followed those turbulent years at the front, full of courage and hardship and high endeavour; and during those years Miss Ogilvy forgot the bad joke that Nature seemed to have played her. She was given the rank of a French lieutenant and she lived in a kind of blissful illusion; appalling reality lay on all sides and yet she managed to live in illusion. She was competent, fearless, devoted and untiring. What then? Could any man hope to do better? She was nearly fifty-eight, yet she walked with a stride, and at times she even swaggered a little.

Poor Miss Ogilvy sitting so glumly in the train with her manly trench-boots and her forage-cap! Poor all the Miss Ogilvies back from the war with their tunics, their trench-boots, and their childish illusions! Wars come and wars go but the world does not change: it will always forget an indebtedness which it thinks it expedient not to remember.

3

When Miss Ogilvy returned to her home in Surrey it was only to find that her sisters were ailing from the usual imaginary causes, and this to a woman who had seen the real thing was intolerable, so that she looked with distaste at Sarah and then at Fanny. Fanny was certainly not prepossessing, she was suffering from a spurious attack of hay fever.

"Stop sneezing!" commanded Miss Ogilvy, in the voice that had so much impressed the Unit. But as Fanny was not in the least impressed, she naturally went on sneezing.

Miss Ogilvy's desk was piled mountain-high with endless tiresome letters and papers: circulars, bills, months-old correspondence, the gardener's accounts, an agent's report on some fields that required land-draining. She seated herself before this collection; then she sighed, it all seemed so absurdly trivial.

"Will you let your hair grow again?" Fanny enquired . . . she and Sarah had followed her into the study. "I'm certain the Vicar would be glad if you did."

"Oh?" murmured Miss Ogilvy, rather too blandly.

"Wilhelmina!"

"Yes?"

"You will do it, won't you?"

"Do what?"

"Let your hair grow; we all wish you would."

"Why should I?"

"Oh, well, it will look less odd, especially now that the war is over—in a small place like this people notice such things."

"I entirely agree with Fanny," announced Sarah.

Sarah had become very self-assertive, no doubt through having mismanaged the estate during the years of her sister's absence. They had quite a heated dispute one morning over the south herbaceous border.

"Whose garden is this?" Miss Ogilvy asked sharply. "I insist on auricula-eyed sweet-williams! I even took the trouble to write from France, but it seems that my letter has been ignored."

"Don't shout," rebuked Sarah, "you're not in France now!"

Miss Ogilvy could gladly have boxed her ears: "I only wish to God I were," she muttered.

Another dispute followed close on its heels, and this time it happened to be over the dinner. Sarah and Fanny were living on weeds—at least that was the way Miss Ogilvy put it.

"We've become vegetarians," Sarah said grandly

"You've become two damn tiresome cranks!" snapped their sister.

Now it never had been Miss Ogilvy's way to indulge in acid recriminations, but somehow, these days, she forgot to say: "Oh?" quite so often as expediency demande 1. It may have been Fanny's perpetual sneezing that had got on her nerves; or it may have been Sarah, or the gardener, or the Vicar, or even the canary; though it really did not matter very much what it was just so long as she found a convenient peg upon which to hang her growing irritation.

"This won't do at all," Miss Ogilvy thought sternly, "life's not worth so much fuss, I must pull myself together." But it seemed this was easier said than done; not a day passed without her losing her temper and that over some trifle: "No, this won't do at all—it just mustn't be," she thought sternly.

Everyone pitied Sarah and Fanny: "Such a dreadful, violent old thing," said the neighbours.

But Sarah and Fanny had their revenge: "Poor darling, it's shell-shock, you know," they murmured.

Thus Miss Ogilvy's prowess was whittled away until she herself was beginning to doubt it. Had she ever been that courageous person who had faced death in France with such perfect composure? Had she ever stood tranquilly under fire, without turning a hair, while she issued her orders? Had she ever been treated with marked respect? She herself was beginning to doubt it.

Sometimes she would see an old member of the Unit, a girl who, more faithful to her than the others, would take the trouble to run down to Surrey. These visits, however, were seldom enlivening.

"Oh, well . . . here we are . . ." Miss Ogilvy would mutter.

But one day the girl smiled and shook her blond head: "I'm not—I'm going to be married."

Strange thoughts had come to Miss Ogilvy, unbidden, thoughts that had stayed for many an hour after the girl's departure. Alone in her study she had suddenly shivered, feeling a sense of complete desolation. With cold hands she had lighted a cigarette.

"I must be ill or something," she had mused, as she stared at her trembling fingers.

After this she would sometimes cry out in her sleep, living over in dreams God knows what emotions; returning, maybe, to the battlefields of France. Her hair turned snow-white; it was not unbecoming yet she fretted about it.

"I'm growing very old," she would sigh as she brushed her thick mop before the glass; and then she would peer at her wrinkles.

For now that it had happened she hated being old; it no longer appeared such an easy solution of those difficulties that had always beset her. And this she resented most bitterly, so that she became the prey of self-pity, and of other undesirable states in which the body will torment the mind, and the mind, in its turn, the body. Then Miss Ogilvy straightened her ageing back, in spite of the fact that of late it had ached with muscular rheumatism, and she faced herself squarely and came to a resolve.

"I'm off!" she announced abruptly one day; and that evening she packed her kit-bag.

4

Near the south coast of Devon there exists a small island that is still very little known to the world, but which, nevertheless, can boast an hotel; the only building upon it. Miss Ogilvy had chosen this place quite at random, it was marked on her map by scarcely more than a dot, but somehow she

17

had liked the look of that dot and had set forth alone to explore it.

She found herself standing on the mainland one morning looking at a vague blur of green through the mist, a vague blur of green that rose out of the Channel like a tidal wave suddenly suspended. Miss Ogilvy was filled with a sense of adventure; she had not felt like this since the ending of the war.

"I was right to come here, very right indeed. I'm going to shake off all my troubles," she decided.

A fisherman's boat was parting the mist, and before it was properly beached, in she bundled.

"I hope they're expecting me?" she said gaily.

"They du be expecting you," the man answered.

The sea, which is generally rough off that coast, was indulging itself in an oily ground-swell; the broad, glossy swells struck the side of the boat, then broke and sprayed over Miss Ogilvy's ankles.

The fisherman grinned: "Feeling all right?" he queried. "It du be tiresome most times about these parts." But the mist had suddenly drifted away and Miss Ogilvy was staring wide-eyed at the island.

She saw a long shoal of jagged black rocks, and

18

between them the curve of a small sloping beach, and above that the lift of the island itself, and above that again, blue heaven. Near the beach stood the little two-storied hotel which was thatched, and built entirely of timber; for the rest she could make out no signs of life apart from a host of white seagulls.

Then Miss Ogilvy said a curious thing. She said: "On the south-west side of that place there was once a cave—a very large cave. I remember that it was some way from the sea."

"There du be a cave still," the fisherman told her, "but it's just above highwater level."

"A-ah," murmured Miss Ogilvy thoughtfully, as though to herself; then she looked embarrassed.

The little hotel proved both comfortable and clean, the hostess both pleasant and comely. Miss Ogilvy started unpacking her bag, changed her mind and went for a stroll round the island. The island was covered with turf and thistles and traversed by narrow green paths thick with daisies. It had four rock-bound coves of which the south-western was by far the most difficult of access. For just here the island descended abruptly as though it were hurtling down to the water; and just here the shale was most treacherous and the tide-swept rocks most aggressively pointed. Here it was that the seagulls, grown fearless of man by reason of his absurd limitations, built their nests on the ledges and reared countless young who multiplied, in their turn, every season. Yes, and here it was that Miss Ogilvy, greatly marvelling, stood and stared across at a cave; much too near the crumbling edge for her safety, but by now completely indifferent to caution.

"I remember . . . I remember . . ." she kept repeating. Then: "That's all very well, but what do I remember?"

She was conscious of somehow remembering all wrong, of her memory being distorted and coloured—perhaps by the endless things she had seen since her eyes had last rested upon that cave. This worried her sorely, far more than the fact that she should be remembering the cave at all, she who had never set foot on the island before that actual morning. Indeed, except for the sense of wrongness when she struggled to piece her memories together, she was steeped in a very profound contentment which surged over her spirit, wave upon wave.

"It's extremely odd," pondered Miss Ogilvy. Then she laughed, so pleased did she feel with its oddness.

5

That night after supper she talked to her hostess who was only too glad, it seemed, to be questioned. She owned the whole island and was proud of the fact, as she very well might be, decided her boarder. Some curious things had been found on the island, according to comely Mrs. Nanceskivel: bronze arrow-heads, pieces of ancient stone celts; and once they had dug up a man's skull and thigh-bone—this had happened while they were sinking a well. Would Miss Ogilvy care to have a look at the bones? They were kept in a cupboard in the scullery.

Miss Ogilvy nodded.

"Then I'll fetch him this moment," said Mrs. Nanceskivel, briskly.

In less than two minutes she was back with the box that contained those poor remnants of a man, and Miss Ogilvy, who had risen from her chair, was gazing down at those remnants. As she did so her mouth was sternly compressed, but her face and her neck flushed darkly.

Mrs. Nanceskivel was pointing to the skull: "Look, miss, he was killed," she remarked rather proudly, "and they tell me that the axe that killed him was bronze. He's thousands and thousands of years old, they tell me. Our local doctor knows a lot about such things and he wants me to send these bones to an expert; they ought to belong to the Nation, he says. But I know what would happen, they'd come digging up my island, and I won't have people digging up my island, I've got enough worry with the rabbits as it is." But Miss Ogilvy could no longer hear the words for the pounding of the blood in her temples.

She was filled with a sudden, inexplicable fury against the innocent Mrs. Nanceskivel: "You . . . *you* . . ." she began, then checked herself, fearful of what she might say to the woman.

For her sense of outrage was overwhelming as she stared at those bones that were kept in the scullery; moreover, she knew how such men had been buried, which made the outrage seem all the more shameful. They had buried such men in deep, well-dug pits surmounted by four stout stones at their corners—four stout stones there had been and a covering stone. And all this Miss Ogilvy knew as by instinct, having no concrete knowledge on which to draw. But she knew it right down in the depths of her soul, and she hated Mrs. Nanceskivel.

And now she was swept by another emotion that was even more strange and more devastating:

22

such a grief as she had not conceived could exist; a terrible unassuageable grief, without hope, without respite, without palliation, so that with something akin to despair she touched the long gash in the skull. Then her eyes, that had never wept since her childhood, filled slowly with large, hot, difficult tears. She must blink very hard, then close her eyelids, turn away from the lamp and say rather loudly:

"Thanks, Mrs. Nanceskivel. It's past eleven— I think I'll be going upstairs."

6

Miss Ogilvy closed the door of her bedroom, after which she stood quite still to consider: "Is it shell-shock?" she muttered incredulously. "I wonder, can it be shell-shock?"

She began to pace slowly about the room, smoking a Caporal. As usual her hands were deep in her pockets; she could feel small, familiar things in those pockets and she gripped them, glad of their presence. Then all of a sudden she was terribly tired, so tired that she flung herself down on the bed, unable to stand any longer.

She thought that she lay there struggling to

reason, that her eyes were closed in the painful effort, and that as she closed them she continued to puff the inevitable cigarette. At least that was what she thought at one moment—the next, she was out in a sunset evening, and a large red sun was sinking slowly to the rim of a distant sea.

Miss Ogilvy knew that she was herself, that is to say she was conscious of her being, and yet she was not Miss Ogilvy at all, nor had she a memory of her. All that she now saw was very familiar, all that she now did was what she should do, and all that she now was seemed perfectly natural. Indeed, she did not think of these things; there seemed no reason for thinking about them.

She was walking with bare feet on turf that felt springy and was greatly enjoying the sensation; she had always enjoyed it, ever since as an infant she had learned to crawl on this turf. On either hand stretched rolling green uplands, while at her back she knew that there were forests; but in front, far away, lay the gleam of the sea towards which the big sun was sinking. The air was cool and intensely still, with never so much as a ripple or bird-song. It was wonderfully pure—one might almost say young—but Miss Ogilvy thought of it merely as air. Having always breathed it she took it for granted, as she took the soft turf and the uplands.

She pictured herself as immensely tall; she was feeling immensely tall at that moment. As a matter of fact she was five feet eight which, however, was quite a considerable height when compared to that of her fellow-tribesmen. She was wearing a single garment of pelts which came to her knees and left her arms sleeveless. Her arms and her legs, which were closely tattooed with blue zig-zag lines, were extremely hairy. From a leathern thong twisted about her waist there hung a clumsily made stone weapon, a celt, which in spite of its clumsiness was strongly hafted and useful for killing.

Miss Ogilvy wanted to shout aloud from a glorious sense of physical well-being, but instead she picked up a heavy, round stone which she hurled with great force at some distant rocks.

"Good! Strong!" she exclaimed. "See how far it goes!"

"Yes, strong. There is no one so strong as you. You are surely the strongest man in our tribe," replied her little companion.

Miss Ogilvy glanced at this little companion and rejoiced that they two were alone together. The girl at her side had a smooth brownish skin, oblique black eyes and short, sturdy limbs. Miss Ogilvy marvelled because of her beauty. She also was wearing a single garment of pelts, new pelts, she had made it that morning. She had stitched at it diligently for hours with short lengths of gut and her best bone needle. A strand of black hair hung over her bosom, and this she was constantly stroking and fondling; then she lifted the strand and examined her hair.

"Pretty," she remarked with childish complacence.

"Pretty," echoed the young man at her side.

"For you," she told him, "all of me is for you and none other. For you this body has ripened."

He shook back his own coarse hair from his eyes; he had sad brown eyes like those of a monkey. For the rest he was lean and steel-strong of loin, broad of chest, and with features not too uncomely. His prominent cheekbones were set rather high, his nose was blunt, his jaw somewhat bestial; but his mouth, though full-lipped, contradicted his jaw, being very gentle and sweet in expression. And now he smiled, showing big, square, white teeth.

"You . . . woman," he murmured contentedly, and the sound seemed to come from the depths of his being.

His speech was slow and lacking in words when it came to expressing a vital emotion, so one word must suffice and this he now spoke, and the word that he spoke had a number of meanings. It meant: "Little spring of exceedingly pure water." It meant: "Hut of peace for a man after battle." It meant: "Ripe red berry sweet to the taste." It meant: "Happy small home of future generations." All these things he must try to express by a word, and because of their loving she understood him.

They paused, and lifting her up he kissed her. Then he rubbed his large shaggy head on her shoulder; and when he released her she knelt at his feet.

"My master; blood of my body," she whispered. For with her it was different, love had taught her love's speech, so that she might turn her heart into sounds that her primitive tongue could utter.

After she had pressed her lips to his hands, and her cheek to his hairy and powerful forearm, she stood up and they gazed at the setting sun, but with bowed heads, gazing under their lids, because this was very sacred.

A couple of mating bears padded towards them from a thicket, and the female rose to her haunches. But the man drew his celt and menaced the beast, so that she dropped down noiselessly and fled, and her mate also fled, for here was the power that few dared to withstand by day or by night, on the

27

uplands or in the forests. And now from across to the left where a river would presently lose itself in the marshes, came a rhythmical thudding, as a herd of red deer with wide nostrils and starting eyes thundered past, disturbed in their drinking by the bears.

After this the evening returned to its silence, and the spell of its silence descended on the lovers, so that each felt very much alone, yet withal more closely united to the other. But the man became restless under that spell, and he suddenly laughed; then grasping the woman he tossed her above his head and caught her. This he did many times for his own amusement and because he knew that his strength gave her joy. In this manner they played together for a while, he with his strength and she with her weakness. And they cried out, and made many guttural sounds which were meaningless save only to themselves. And the tunic of pelts slipped down from her breasts, and her two little breasts were pear-shaped.

Presently, he grew tired of their playing, and he pointed towards a cluster of huts and earthworks that lay to the eastward. The smoke from these huts rose in thick straight lines, bending neither to right nor left in its rising, and the thought of sweet burning rushes and brushwood touched his consciousness, making him feel sentimental.

"Smoke," he said.

And she answered: "Blue smoke."

He nodded: "Yes, blue smoke—home."

Then she said: "I have ground much corn since the full moon. My stones are too smooth. You make me new stones."

"All you have need of, I make," he told her.

She stole closer to him, taking his hand: "My father is still a black cloud full of thunder. He thinks that you wish to be head of our tribe in his place, because he is now very old. He must not hear of these meetings of ours, if he did I think he would beat me!"

So he asked her: "Are you unhappy, small berry?"

But at this she smiled: "What is being unhappy? I do not know what that means any more."

"I do not either," he answered.

Then as though some invisible force had drawn him, his body swung round and he stared at the forests where they lay and darkened, fold upon fold; and his eyes dilated with wonder and terror, and he moved his head quickly from side to side as a wild thing will do that is held between bars and whose mind is pitifully bewildered.

29

"Water!" he cried hoarsely, "great water—look, look! Over there. This land is surrounded by water!"

"What water?" she questioned.

He answered: "The sea." And he covered his face with his hands.

"Not so," she consoled, "big forests, good hunting. Big forests ın which you hunt boar and aurochs. No sea over there but only the trees."

He took his trembling hands from his face: "You are right . . . only trees," he said dully.

But now his face had grown heavy and brooding and he started to speak of a thing that oppressed him: "The Roundheaded-ones, they are devils," he growled, while his bushy black brows met over his eyes, and when this happened it changed his expression which became a little sub-human.

"No matter," she protested, for she saw that he forgot her and she wished him to think and talk only of love. "No matter. My father laughs at your fears. Are we not friends with the Round-headed-ones? We are friends, so why should we fear them?"

"Our forts, very old, very weak," he went on, "and the Roundheaded-ones have terrible weapons. Their weapons are not made of good stone like ours, but of some dark, devilish substance."

"What of that?" she said lightly. "They would fight on our side, so why need we trouble about their weapons?"

But he looked away, not appearing to hear her. "We must barter all, all for their celts and arrows and spears, and then we must learn their secret. They lust after our women, they lust after our lands. We must barter all, all for their sly brown celts."

"Me . . . bartered?" she queried, very sure of his answer otherwise she had not dared to say this.

"The Roundheaded-ones may destroy my tribe and yet I will not part with you," he told her. Then he spoke very gravely: "But I think they desire to slay us, and me they will try to slay first because they well know how much I mistrust them—they have seen my eyes fixed many times on their camps."

She cried: "I will bite out the throats of these people if they so much as scratch your skin!"

And at this his mood changed and he roared with amusement: "You . . . woman!" he roared. "Little foolish white teeth. Your teeth were made for nibbling wild cherries, not for tearing the throats of the Roundheaded-ones!"

"Thoughts of war always make me afraid," she whimpered, still wishing him to talk about love.

He turned his sorrowful eyes upon her, the eyes that were sad even when he was merry, and although his mind was often obtuse, yet he clearly perceived how it was with her then. And his blood caught fire from the flame in her blood, so that he strained her against his body.

"You . . . mine . . ." he stammered.

"Love," she said, trembling, "this is love."

And he answered: "Love."

Then their faces grew melancholy for a moment, because dimly, very dimly in their dawning souls, they were conscious of a longing for something more vast than this earthly passion could compass.

Presently, he lifted her like a child and carried her quickly southward and westward till they came to a place where a gentle descent led down to a marshy valley. Far away, at the line where the marshes ended, they discerned the misty line of the sea; but the sea and the marshes were become as one substance, merging, blending, folding to- gether; and since they were lovers they also would be one, even as the sea and the marshes.

And now they had reached the mouth of a cave that was set in the quiet hillside. There was bright green verdure beside the cave, and a number of small, pink, thick-stemmed flowers that when they were crushed smelt of spices. And within the cave there was bracken newly gathered and heaped together for a bed; while beyond, from some rocks, came a low liquid sound as a spring dripped out through a crevice. Abruptly, he set the girl on her feet, and she knew that the days of her innocence were over. And she thought of the anxious virgin soil that was rent and sown to bring forth fruit in season, and she gave a quick little gasp of fear:

"No . . . no . . ." she gasped. For, divining his need, she was weak with the longing to be possessed, yet the terror of love lay heavy upon her. "No . . . no . . ." she gasped.

But he caught her wrist and she felt the great strength of his rough, gnarled fingers, the great strength of the urge that leapt in his loins, and again she must give that quick gasp of fear, the while she clung close to him lest he should spare her.

The twilight was engulfed and possessed by darkness, which in turn was transfigured by the moonrise, which in turn was fulfilled and consumed by dawn. A mighty eagle soared up from his eyrie, cleaving the air with his masterful wings, and beneath him from the rushes that harboured their nests, rose other great birds, crying loudly. Then the heavy-horned elks appeared on the uplands, bending their burdened heads to the sod; while beyond in the forests the fierce wild aurochs stamped as they bellowed their love songs.

But within the dim cave the lord of these creatures had put by his weapon and his instinct for slaying. And he lay there defenceless with tenderness, thinking no longer of death but of life as he murmured the word that had so many meanings. That meant: "Little spring of exceedingly pure water." That meant: "Hut of peace for a man after battle." That meant: "Ripe red berry sweet to the taste." That meant: "Happy small home of future generations."

7

They found Miss Ogilvy the next morning; the fisherman saw her and climbed to the ledge. She was sitting at the mouth of the cave. She was dead, with her hands thrust deep into her pockets.

THE LOVER OF THINGS

I

MRS. DOBBS was not an affectionate
mother; small wonder, perhaps, considering her
means and the size of her family. Mr. Dobbs had
possessed a versatile mind, a liking for liquor, and
an amorous nature. Jack of all trades and master of
none, he had drifted from badly paid job to job
until double pneumonia had closed his career
when Henry was just eleven.

There were four other children all under that
age; an ill-fed, ill-tempered, ill-washed lot who
quarrelled and howled in and out of season—this
because they had many small bodily woes and were
not infrequently hungry. Mrs. Dobbs charred
every day of the week and sewed every evening,
when fate was propitious, and yet there was never
enough to eat, never quite enough, which made it
so hopeless, and her thoughts would dwell on the
late Mr. Dobbs with malevolence:

"Don't talk to me about men, dirty, stinkin'
'ounds, we all knows what they wants when
they comes round a woman . . . it's always the
same . . ." And then she might clap her hand

to her back with a groan, remembering her floating kidney.

But although she had no time to waste on affection, no time to waste on anything but slaps and querulous abuse, yet she deeply resented the aloofness displayed by her eldest son; an aloofness that seemed to set him apart from her gruelling struggle for existence. Not that Henry was "bad" as Mrs. Dobbs put it, quite the contrary, Henry was nearly always good, but his goodness had a negative quality about it.

" 'E's only bein' good 'cause 'e don't *feel* bad," she would think with rising irritation.

His brothers and sister she found more natural— there was certainly nothing aloof about them as they fought and yelled, or whimpered and lied. They spent most of their time in the neighbouring gutters where, occasionally, they tormented a cat, or a puppy if one chanced to be handy. But Henry, her first-born, had never yelled except for a few weeks during his teething; he never picked quarrels, never complained, never troubled himself to tell her a lie, never took the least interest in cats or puppies. Amiable, but alien, he went his own way; there were times when he seemed to her scarcely human.

In appearance, also, he was unlike the others:

they were small and puny, whereas, at eleven
Henry was exceedingly big for his age, with a
healthy body that would not stop growing. His
thick hair was black whereas theirs was sandy, his
hazel eyes bright whereas theirs lacked lustre. For
the rest his face was coarse-featured and strong,
rather set in expression for so young a boy,
possibly because he smiled very seldom.

But apart from these physical characteristics,
which appeared to his mother to be those of a
stranger, Henry had a habit that she greatly
disliked: Mrs. Dobbs would sometimes glance up
from her work to find him staring out into space,
and his eyes would look blank.

"It fair gives me the 'ump," she must often
confide to a neighbour.

If her back were aching she might shout at her
son: "Stop that daft look, sittin' there glarin' at
nothin'! Stop it, I tell yer, or I'll box yer ears!"
And Henry would dutifully stop his staring.

He was seldom perturbed by her threats or her
blows, this because, to him, she mattered so little,
so much less than a number of other things—the
squalid house he lived in, for instance. The house
always seemed to Henry more real, more alive, and
thus more compelling of notice. When he had
banged its blistered front door, he might mutter:

"Ugly . . . 'orribly ugly!" And then to the street with its dismal rows of equally poor and neglected houses: "Ugly! Ugly! I 'ates yer all!" In this manner he sometimes relieved his feelings.

But ugly was not quite expressive enough, so one morning at school he consulted his teacher: "Hi, Miss!"

"Yes, Henry?"

"What's worse than ugly? What's more like our house?"

Without thinking Miss Selby suggested: "Hideous." Then blushing, she frowned: "But you mustn't interrupt in the middle of class —of course your home is not hideous," she told him.

"Is hijous uglier than ugly?" he persisted.

"Yes, hideous means something. . . . well, rather dreadful."

"Thank you, Miss," said Henry, quite satisfied; and he scribbled the new word down in his note-book.

2

He was not a good student. He was patient and docile, but apparently always lacking in interest.

Mrs. Dobbs explained this by what she described as: "That 'abit of 'is of scourin' the streets." And for once she was right in her explanation.

Henry did scour the streets; not the dreary-faced alleys that clung like grey mould round the house of his mother, but the busy and wealthy streets of the west through which flowed the mighty gold-stream of London. He would come home from school, put his satchel on the dresser, and then padding across to the sink would wash his hands. All his movements were large and quiet and sure, yet with something ungainly and bearlike about them. His hands washed he would go out, and once free of the house and the street he would draw a deep breath of contentment. Perhaps he would know the direction of his goal but perhaps he would not, and when this latter happened he would feel like a man who sailed uncharted seas, and his pulses would quicken with a sense of adventure.

Windows, shop-windows, windows of things! Wonderful caskets of glass full of treasures at which Henry Dobbs could stand spellbound—gazing. He could press his palms to the thick, cold panes and feel their texture against his skin, imagining the while how those other things felt: the glossy mahogany, satin-wood and walnut; the lovely, mysterious, grey-brown oak that looked so old and so restful. Not that he knew the names of those woods that dead craftsmen had once forced into their service, but he sensed in an inarticulate way the joy that such men must have found in their craft, in creating, possessing and handling beauty.

"Gor' blimey," Henry would sigh as he gazed; and this was the only prayer that he knew, for Mrs. Dobbs had long since done with praying.

But windows, more windows, and in some would be pictures—pictures of flowers and of dim, lovely landscapes; pictures of ships with billowing sails; pictures of strangely dressed, grand-looking people; pictures of pleasant but curious rooms; pictures of cities very different from London. Pictures, yes, but windows of other things too: of stones that glowed with marvellous colours. These were jewels, Henry had learnt this much by closely observing the ladies who wore them, and he did not like to see precious stones worn, it gave him a queerly resentful feeling, not because of his own extreme poverty, but rather because of the jewels themselves.

"They can't abide it, I knows as they can't," he would muse, "they don't want to be messed up with bodies."

His lack of knowledge irked him at this time, for he longed to be intimate with his treasures, longed

42

to speak to them through those barriers of glass, yet would never feel sure by what names to call them. Those queer little blue-green boxes, for instance, they greatly allured him, but what were they made of? He stared fascinated at such a box in the window of a shop in New Bond Street one evening.

"That's a jolly good bit of shagreen," came a voice as a man's hand pointed over his shoulder.

"Yes," answered another man, "jolly good."

Henry swung round: "What's shagreen?" he demanded, "is it the stuff of that there box?"

The men looked surprised, then one of them laughed: "It is, my bright lad, and shagreen is shark's skin. Can I give you any further assistance?"

"Yeh," said Henry promptly. But the men strolled away. "Shagreen . . ." he pondered. "I likes that word; it sounds, it sounds, it sounds. . . rare," he decided.

In the end he picked up a good deal of information by listening to his fellow-window-shoppers. Learned, for instance, to recognise Dresden china; learned that some things were fashioned in a substance called bronze, and that others were carved from ivory, while yet others were hewn out of stuff called marble. He learned the words: Gothic and Tudor oak, in connection with certain old chests and tables. And one day he learned the proud word, brocade, from a lady who stood admiring that fabric. Thus, little by little his mind began to grow in proportion to his growing knowledge of language and he talked to himself of the things he loved, murmuring their names softly under his breath as though by so doing he could summon them to him.

But they never came, and it was not enough any longer merely to stand there gazing; he desired too intensely the pleasure of touch, so would sometimes wander to the humbler shops where antiques were often displayed on the pavement. Very reverently he would pat and stroke, filled with a deep delight at the contact. But as likely as not the salesman would catch him.

"Now then, what are you doing? Stop that!" he might shout.

And Henry would turn away shaking his head: "Bloody fool," he would mutter, "I knows 'ow to touch 'em . . ."

3

At thirteen he left school, an outstanding example of how well-meaning statesmen can waste public money. He had learned to read and to write; beyond this young Henry had contrived to learn very little.

His presence in the home proved no unmixed blessing; he was growing morose with his sister and brothers, while Mrs. Dobbs found him intolerably large—he would seem to fill her small kitchen to bursting. Indeed, he possessed but one virtue in her eyes: he could always be trusted with fragile objects, and could thus be made to wash up after meals.

" 'Ow yer manages it I don't know," she would say, "with them great 'ams of 'ands."

And Henry would feel that his bigness made his mother dislike him.

Yet it certainly was surprising to see those ungainly hands touching china and glass as delicately as some Georgian lady's. Nothing that Henry washed ever broke, his fingers automatically took the right angle, the angle that held with complete confidence, the angle that made his grasp firm but gentle. And so it would be with most other things; he could move a table that had a loose leg and the leg would remain in position for Henry; he could lift a chair with a rickety back and the chair would hold its back upright for Henry. Oh, yes, Henry could always be trusted with things if he could not now always be trusted with people.

His handling of people was much less considerate; he never intentionally hurt a person, because he had no real desire to hurt, but he shoved the children out of his way, and even at thirteen his shoves were potent. Or, perhaps he would blunder onto a corn that was filling his mother with untold anguish, or bump clumsily into pedestrians in his haste to arrive at those plate-glass windows. Sometimes he said: "Sorry," but more often he did not, which was natural, perhaps, since he never felt sorry. In subtler ways, also, he lacked imagination when it came to the matter of human relations; thus the year he left school and should have found work he made not the slightest effort to find it. Mrs. Dobbs grew very angry indeed, and her anger would vent itself on him at meal times.

"Eatin' yer 'ead off, yer great lazy lump. No yer don't 'ave another 'elp!" she would scream.

And Henry might sigh but would never complain; he possessed a kind of heavy endurance.

The meals had been growing sparser of late, and the four younger children now never stopped puling. Mrs. Dobbs had lost her daily job and had not yet succeeded in finding another; small wonder that she jibed at her eldest son, and had come to begrudge him his every mouthful. As a matter of fact he was not at all greedy, but to see him lounging there at the table, and he not lifting a finger to help at this time of acute anxiety, would have tried any ailing and anxious parent, and it tried Mrs. Dobbs till she nearly went mad.

"Gawd, if it wasn't for me kidney what's loose, I'd thrash the 'ide off yer lazy back! I'd teach yer to live on me!" she would tell him.

Yet he had his good points: he never stole food when his mother was out, though he often felt hungry. The others did steal when they got the chance and when there was anything left in the cupboard. Henry did not blame them, he never blamed, though he often felt sorry; not because of the children who were driven by their hunger to theft, but rather because of some inanimate thing that had recently gripped his imagination.

He would think: "Now supposin' that Toodor table what I seed, was standin' 'ere in this room— I'd 'ate it to see young Tom pinchin' cheese." And then he would try to picture the table in its original surroundings.

But in this he would fail ignominiously—he had been a careless student of history. All the same a dumb pity would surge up in his heart, a pity vaguely connected with the house, with the street, with the times in which they must live:

"Good Lord," he would think, "couldn't let it come 'ere—this kitchen ain't fit for an old Toodor table."

Yet he felt no shame, and that was so strange, no shame that urged him to get out and earn. Even when Mrs. Dobbs wept one evening, when she covered her face with her apron and wept, rocking her body backwards and forwards; even when she uncovered her face and stared with desperate eyes at her son, he only stared back at her stupidly as though he were lacking in comprehension.

"You just standin' there gapin' at me," she blubbered; "you just standin' there doin' nothin' at all. . . . 'Ow can I go and find yer a job, and me not closin' an eye of nights what with me corns and this pain in me back. Wantin' to live off yer mother, yer are; 'tain't natural, it's you as oughter be workin', 'stead of which yer must go round scourin' the streets. What is it yer does all them hours in the streets? It's cruel 'ard, an' me feelin' like death . . ."

He fidgeted, thinking how ugly she looked, how hideous—yes, hideous, that was the word—Miss Selby had said that it meant more than ugly.

"Can't yer say summat, 'Enry?" she sobbed.

But he honestly did not know what to say, for how could he put his thoughts into words? If he did so, in spite of her back she would strike him. He was thinking: "Shops . . . them things in the windows. 'Ow late would I 'ave to work at a job? Would they keep me until they puts up the shutters . . . till they puts out the lights? If I found a job, 'ow early would I 'ave to get there of mornin's . . . before I could take a look at them things? Gawd, I might never be able to see 'em!"

Mrs. Dobbs got up, groaning: "Well, I'm goin' to me bed." And she took the kettle with her to soak her corns.

Henry gazed after her thin bent back and he frowned: "Wish she'd let me alone . . ." he muttered.

4

It could not go on. Henry's sister was ill. She had scabs that covered her face and scalp. They said that the child must not attend school until she was cured—malnutrition, they called it. Thomas, for all his thieving of cheese, caught a cold that quickly turned to bronchitis; more trouble and yet more, things were grim indeed, and one morning they suddenly came to a climax. Mrs. Dobbs pinned on her rusty black hat. She must risk being late for a new office job, she would have to explain that two children were ill, that her eldest boy was refusing to work—she would just have to risk it and try to explain. She made for the stationer's shop round the corner.

The stationer had known the late Mr. Dobbs and was therefore disposed to pity his widow: "Yes," he said thoughtfully, scratching his beard, "I might give young Henry a bit of a trial; I'm wanting a lad to deliver papers. But mind you, he'll have to be punctual and sprack, no dawdling about or he gets the boot. Still, I'd like to give you a helping hand; the youngster can start in to-morrow morning."

That evening Mrs. Dobbs confronted her son: "You'll go for them papers at cockscrow ter-morrer. And mind that yer delivers 'em right; if yer don't, I'll get Mr. Wilkins to thrash yer, so yer needn't go thinkin' that because I'm weak yer'll be gettin' off this time. Understand what I says? Yer'll do as 'e orders!"

Henry nodded.

5

Henry's beat lay round Fulham Road and Chelsea, among a number of well-kept houses and a few less well-kept maisonettes and studios. With a bundle of dailies in an old canvas bag he now sallied forth to ring bells and thump knockers, and this part of the business he did not dislike. The shops being still asleep at that hour, there was nothing else that he wanted to do and thumping the knockers was rather amusing.

Having lived in a slum off the Fulham Road all his life, he knew every short cut in the district, and could thus quickly finish his morning's work and return home again for his meagre breakfast. But as Gertie continued to scratch her scabs, and as Thomas continued excessively ailing, Mrs. Dobbs had forbidden him to leave the house until she returned to prepare the dinner, so that Henry must loll about kicking his heels, ostensibly in charge of the children. After dinner he was free, and therein lay the snag, for at five-thirty sharp he must be at his post to prepare for the evening delivery, and Henry was nearly always unpunctual. Having gone far afield in search of romance and forgotten the time, he would start to run, only to find himself snared anew by the antique shops of the King's Road, Chelsea. Customers complained, as customers will when something occurs which is not to their liking, and but for the stationer's charity, Mrs. Dobbs would have found the boy

back on her hands; as it was, Mr. Wilkins boxed
Henry's ears with Henry's mother's whole-hearted
approval.

One only of Mr. Wilkins's customers possessed
the slightest interest for Henry, and this was not
because of himself but because of a certain Gothic
chest which happened to be in the young man's
possession. The owner of the chest lived in
Manresa Road, in a dirty, neglected ground-floor
studio, but he himself was exceedingly neat, and
was much addicted to gaudy pyjamas. Every
morning he would come to the grimy front door
when Henry knocked, and would take in his
paper.

"Hallo, you!" he would grin good-humouredly.

Then Henry would grin: "Hallo, yerself!" but
his eyes would stray to the old Gothic chest that
occupied most of the tiny lobby.

Very fine it was, elaborately carved yet appearing
both dignified and simple. Its colour was of that
indescribable tone which is so greatly prized by
earnest collectors; its original lock-plate was well-
preserved, and even its key was a thing of beauty.
But alas, who, or what may escape from time?
Not even a great-hearted Gothic chest, and this
splendid veteran was feeling its years, for the
worms were eating into its entrails. Nevertheless,

its face remained brave, and Henry was conscious of this dumb courage, so that he blurted out loudly one day:

"Mister, I wants to touch that chest!"

Joe Millington paused in lighting his pipe. His fair eyebrows shot up in a quizzical line as he glanced at the clumsy, unkempt oaf who delivered his papers: "Go on, then," he said kindly.

It was raining, but Henry forgot this fact, and down went his papers in the mud of the door-step. Very softly he padded across to the chest and ran his hand over its rippling surface. Millington, watching the boy's grimy face, described it afterwards as ecstatic.

"Gothic, ain't it?" Henry enquired, looking up.

Joe Millington laughed and nodded his head: "I believe so, but what do you know about Gothic?"

"I seed a chest somethin' like this one day, and a man come along and called it that—Gothic's an easy word to remember."

The artist was amused: "Have some coffee," he suggested. "You're drenched."

"Don't mind if I do," agreed Henry.

The studio was fuggy. It smelt of paint, stale cigarette smoke and last night's whisky. At one end stood a rakish-looking divan, a shaving-stand, and an unemptied sitz-bath; in the middle of the floor stood a battered easel. But coming in out of the cold and rain, not only to coffee but to hot rolls and butter, Henry suddenly sighed as a soul might sigh that had unexpectedly entered Heaven.

"Sit down and devour," commanded his host, "go on, eat till you bust! You seem pretty hungry."

Presently, Millington ventured a question: "Do you like old oak?" he asked very gravely.

Henry's mouth was full, but he managed to speak: "I more nor like it, Mister, I loves it." Then because he felt that Millington might understand: "But I loves all them other things too—you know—figures, and little shagreen boxes and things. . . ."

"I see. In fact you're a connoisseur."

"Don't know what yer mean. Yer not kiddin' me, are yer?"

"Of course not. But where have you seen such boxes?"

Henry washed down a chunk of roll, then he said: "I makes it my business to look into winders."

Millington was now more than ever diverted. A gutter-snipe with the soul of a Duveen and the appetite of a starving grampus. He stared at

Henry's great frost-cracked hands that had touched the chest with such delicacy, and his interest grew; perhaps he would paint him, perhaps he would create an abstract of this boy, portraying his strange emotional curves. He would call the picture: "The Gothic Chest." Yes, but leave the chest out—that would be intriguing. Curves began to excite then obsess his brain, together with stark, disconcerting lines . . . subtlety and crudity, weakness and strength. . . .

"Would you like to look at my pictures?" he enquired, curious to see how his guest would react.

They went round the studio. Henry was silent.

At last: "Is it possible," Millington asked him, "is it possible that you don't care for my pictures?" And he grinned.

"They're bloody!" Henry burst out rudely. The moment the words were spoken he trembled, horrified and amazed at his awful daring, but the pictures had filled him with sudden rage, so that he continued to babble: "If you paints them things then you can't love it."

"What's 'it'?" queried Millington, still amused.

Henry pointed to the lobby.

"Oh, I see—the chest. Well, I don't know why not; I'm very broad-minded. You aren't, I observe."

Henry shook his head. His rage died down abruptly; he felt ill at ease.

"Come now, can't you see any beauty in my work?"

"I can't see nothin' at all," muttered Henry.

How he longed to lie; but somehow he could not, for he felt that the eyes of the chest were upon him as he stood near the open studio door, that the chest had ears and was anxiously listening; that the chest had a heart that was beating very fast, that the chest was alive and in need of help, his help. And there came upon Henry Dobbs the first faint understanding of chivalry.

"It's that what I loves 'cause it can't 'elp itself, and it 'ates bein' 'ere with you," he protested.

Millington smiled at him tolerantly: "Perhaps. But I wouldn't get all balled-up over a mouldy old Gothic has-been. Now, out you go, kid, I've got to work. I think I shall make an abstract of you. Come again some day soon and eat hot buttered rolls—and jam," he added.

"I dunno," frowned Henry.

*   *   *   *   *

All the way back down Manresa Road Henry was lost in unhappy meditation. If only he could rescue the Gothic chest from that smiling young man in the striped silk pyjamas. The chest was unloved and it needed love. It was compelled to live near those hideous pictures. It belonged to a man who despised its great age, who had dared to call it a Gothic has-been.

If only he, Henry, were powerful and rich, he would force its hateful owner to sell it. Or suppose he were the boss of some desperate gang, he would then break into the house with his men and carry the Gothic chest into safety. But one thing, he decided, he would never do again: he would never again eat hot buttered rolls with Millington; never, no, never again, not even if Millington bribed him with jam, not even if he were terribly hungry.

He wandered on and on in the rain; his shoulders drooped, his face sullen and heavy. For the first time he realised poverty—it was terrible not to be able to help a thing that one loved, a thing that was helpless. He sighed a large, deep-drawn and painful sigh, then he wondered how often the old chest sighed as it stood in that cramped and dirty lobby. When at last he got home the dinner was over and his mother eyed him with weary resentment, and still with resentment she fetched him his food.

"Wet to the skin yer are," she grumbled, not

57　　　　　　　　　　B

offering to dry his rain-drenched clothes, "now come on, make 'aste with that there plate of stoo. Yer brother's coughin' somethin' awful again and I needs the plate for 'is linseed poultice. Not that you'd care if we all dropped down dead! Why wasn't yer 'ere to look after young Tommy? Yer 'aven't got as much 'eart as a bug, or else yer potty . . . maybe it's that . . ." and opening the cupboard she got out the linseed.

He went on gloomily eating his dinner, hunching his back, sopping up the gravy with hunks of bread and then licking his fingers. Let her rage, he cared nothing for her abuse, less than nothing, except that it made her more ugly. Then quite suddenly his face became blank:

"Gawd Almighty!" he shouted, leaping to his feet. "Gawd Almighty! if I ain't forgot all me papers!"

"Yer what?" squealed Mrs. Dobbs, spinning round.

"Me papers, the 'ole blasted bundle of 'em, the 'ole bundle! I'd only delivered three!"

For once Mrs. Dobbs found no adequate words, she was smitten dumb with horror and fury; but she snatched away what was left of his stew and flung it back into the greasy pan, after which she struck him with all her might on the cheek, then sank heavily into a chair.

"That kidney o' mine do be achin'," she whined, her anger submerged in a tide of self-pity.

He pressed his hand to his smarting face. His eyes held in them no trace of resentment, but no compassion—that kidney of hers had been aching ever since he could remember. Turning, he padded across to the door:

"Be 'ome again presently," he informed her.

Mr. Wilkins met him with six terse words: "You're not wanted here, my lad," he remarked.

"I say, 'old on, there . . ." Henry began.

Mr. Wilkins frowned; he was through with this lout: "You're not wanted here, my lad," he repeated.

"Them papers . . . I left 'em . . ."

"Yes, I know you did. Mr. Millington brought the lot back this morning."

6

Henry was almost happy once more. The local vicar did what he could, but work was extremely scarce that year, so Henry might prowl his favourite streets to his heart's content with no one to coerce him, but his steps often turned to Manresa Road as though drawn by some invisible magnet.

A month passed before he again saw the artist, then they met in the archway that led to the studio: "Hallo, you!" called Joe Millington affably, "I've got the brokers in here—such nice fellows!"

Henry knew all there was to know about brokers, for brokers were his mother's perpetual nightmare. "They drags the very mattress from under yer back and the crust from yer mouth," she was fond of explaining, so that now Henry stared at Joe Millington, aghast.

"But the chest . . . what about that there chest . . ." he faltered.

"They'll take it, I suppose," said the blithe young man. "I believe it's worth a fairly large sum." He surveyed the boy with his humorous eyes, then: "This is what comes of a depraved public taste in art; ever been to Burlington House? Oh! by the way, youngster, those papers of yours . . .."

But Henry left him without a word. The chest, the old chest to be shamed like this, to be seized because Millington couldn't pay the rent; the cowardly betrayal, the outrage of it!

*   *   *   *   *

Henry's nights became restless. He would tumble into bed only to dream that the Gothic chest had found a voice and was crying out to him: "Henry, Henry, save me!" it cried, and Henry would know that he could not save it.

No work, little food, and a bitter cold spring. Henry's imaginings grew apace, he was now obsessed by the strangest fancies whenever he so much as closed his eyes, they would even come when his eyes were wide open. He had crawled into the chest and the lid had shut on him; he was stifling there in the heart of the chest—he would have to die because the chest loved him. He had fondled the beautiful thing so often that his fingers had stiffened, they were gnarled like oak. Crikey! they were oak, he could no longer bend them. He was one of the odd little men in armour whose figures appeared on the front of the chest; he was not Henry Dobbs, he was part of the chest, no doubt this was why they must love each other. If the chest should be chopped up for firewood then he, Henry Dobbs, would have to burn. . . .

His mother observed him with unfriendly eyes: " 'E's got 'is daft look again," she would think. "I can't abide that daft look of 'is—kind of scares me. I do believe the lad's queer." And then she would call on the woman next door, and together they would shake their heads over Henry.

The end came very abruptly one morning. Henry had gone to Manresa Road, where he found a van drawn up outside the studio. The door of the studio had been flung open and Millington's voice reached the boy where he stood.

"Steady the Buffs!" came Millington's voice. Then two other voices, grumbling, morose. Then a thud and Millington's gay voice again: "Oh, well, it's not I who'll be facing the guns, but I warn you that chest's a collector's piece; however, it don't concern me any longer."

Millington was wrapped in a dressing-gown of thick purple brocade: "Hallo, you!" he remarked, greeting Henry with the usual words and grin: "I'm sorry I can't offer refreshments this morning; there's nothing in the larder but the spine of a sardine, some Keating's Powder and a brace of black beetles. However, I'm delighted to see you again, you're just in the nick of time for the funeral."

They were coming, two shabby undersized men grasping the Gothic chest between them. They staggered and paused, breathing stertorously—the chest was still as heavy as iron. They were digging their fingers into its wounds, wounds that the worms had made in its body, and the powder that

62

gushed out seemed to Henry like blood, so that he
wanted to strike at their hands because of the pain
that they were inflicting. The men lurched weakly
towards the door, making ugly sounds as they
strained to their task, and Henry felt certain that
they hated the chest because it was shaming their
puny muscles. Then one of them slipped as he
reached the step and a corner of the chest crashed
down on the stone, and it fell away softly, decayed
and dreadful.

Henry screamed like an hysterical girl: "Damn
you! Damn you! Damn you!" he screamed,
"you've hurt it, you'll kill it, you stinkin' swine!"

The men turned to stare and Millington laughed:
"Never mind, you, it's not mine any more; let them
bang it about, I've no objection."

But Henry was not listening. He had flung off
his coat and now he was lifting the chest himself:
"Come on," he said, rather breathlessly. "I'll 'elp
yer as far as the van, if yer'll let me."

He could feel his own muscles strained to breaking, and he actually prayed that they might not fail;
he had no idea who or what he invoked, but he
felt the need of prayer at that moment.

"Kind of 'Ercules, you are!" panted one of the
men.

Henry scowled at him: "Come on, do!" he

gasped. And again, more faintly: "Come on . . ."

Very slowly they heaved the chest into the van where it stood lopsided among filthy straw, a picture of complete desolation.

Millington remained in the doorway and observed, a Gold Flake gripped between his front teeth. If only he could get this boy to sit: "I say, you!" he began, "I want to have a word . . ."

But Henry ignored that flippant voice. With averted eyes he slipped on his jacket. As he hurried away his mind became clear for the first time in weeks, and he thought that he knew why his body had been made so big and strong —so big and so strong that his mother disliked him.

"It's for liftin' them beautiful 'elpless things, that's why I was born so 'efty," he thought, "I can't 'ave 'em, but just the same I can 'elp 'em and see that they ain't all battered and bruised. That's what I'm for, to 'andle them things quiet and respectful-like, as is proper."

7

It was not until he was twenty years old that Henry obtained employment at Riley's. Mr. Riley would never engage lads too young because of the strain upon immature bodies. Riley's had an almost unique reputation for expert removals and careful warehousing, and was thus the firm most often employed should a well-known collector wish to move his collection. Riley's boast was that they could pack an egg with a ton of bricks, and the egg be unbroken.

Henry had made exhaustive enquiries about them before he had entered their service; he had even loitered around their yard and been ordered off on several occasions, but this not until his sharp eyes had glimpsed the class of goods that they sometimes handled. Meanwhile he had quietly settled down, for six years, to whatever dull jobs had offered; since once having sighted a desirable goal which he might hope to reach were he patient and steady, patient and steady Henry had become.

" 'E's the dead spit of one what's got religion, so changed 'e is," Mrs. Dobbs had declared almost piously, remembering an uncle who had joined the Salvation Army.

At Riley's Henry was known as "the giant." An enormous young man, over six foot four in his socks, and broad in proportion. His face was arresting with its healthy pallor, the hard self-

65

assured reserve of the mouth, and the quick, watchful glance of the hazel eyes that struck one as being attentive yet restless; and then his thick hair which now that he oiled it appeared as blue-black as the hair of a Spaniard. Handsome he was not, and yet there was something about Henry that made women turn to look at him. He might have had several affairs of the heart had he been so disposed, but sexually cold, he had seldom felt more than a passing impulse.

Henry's first removal proved a drab sort of business, concerned with drab and melancholy things from a Bayswater home which they closely resembled; and he learned that even at the celebrated Riley's work could be far from exciting. Moreover, his foreman continually nagged him, regarding his youth with hostile suspicion. Henry must not pack what his foreman called "fragiles," must not touch the clocks or the books or the silver; indeed all that he was permitted to do was to help in shifting the heaviest pieces. His most daring exploit during those days consisted in giving a hand with a piano.

For more than six months nothing came Henry's way that could not have been done, so he thought, by a navvy; then Riley's got the order to move Charles Reide, the South African millionaire, whose

collections of old china, silver and French furniture
were fast becoming world-famous. Henry could
not sleep when he heard the great news. Which
men would they put on the job? What foreman?
An irritating devil, his own foreman, Smith, and
clearly not at all friendly towards him. In any case
Smith and his men might not go—there were fore-
men at Riley's who had seen longer service. Yet
one morning Smith appeared wreathed in smiles,
and Henry could have sworn that he strutted a
little.

"We're picked for that Park Lane millionaire
stunt!" he called across the warehouse to Henry.
Then he spat on his hands and smoothed back his
hair complacently, for no walk in life but is sown
with the nettles of competition.

They started delivering cases on a Monday and
continued to deliver them for two days. On the
third day the men trooped up from the basement
and were given the freedom of the house in Park
Lane, that huge mansion that sheltered the Reide
collections. Henry had never seen anything like
it: the black marble hall with its gleaming fountain,
the splendid reception rooms, vast, austere, containing their cabinets filled with treasures; the
library with its calf-bound books; the study with
its furniture of the First Empire; the master's bed-

room, less vast, less austere, rather womanish in
fact with its Louis Quinze bed and its elegant
chairs upholstered in silk, but having an indis-
putable beauty because of the pale gleam of time-
worn gilt, the harmonious blending of time-worn
fabrics.

"Now then, get a move on!" rasped Smith's
harsh voice. "I ain't brought you to the Zoological
Gardens!"

What an experience it was, that first day; what
an orgy of staring, what an orgy of touching.
Every moment Henry's hands fondled things that
he loved, the feel of which gave him an exquisite
pleasure. If only he had been in charge of the men
his cup of joy must have overflowed, but Smith
it was who ordered the men, and ordered them,
so Henry thought, very badly. Henry watched
them lift with his heart in his mouth, watched them
swing up a priceless chair by its back or distribute
the weight unevenly when they lifted a heavy but
rickety table; watched them jerk a valuable picture
off its nail. Experienced men, they all knew their
job and were not going to bring disgrace on the
firm, but to Henry they seemed like so many
butchers. He shared their labours and did what
he could, realising that he could do very little, and
he marvelled at Smith's imperturbable calm—

Smith did not appear in the least apprehensive.

"If only I was the boss," Henry thought. Then he thought: "Some day I will be the boss—I bloody well mean to get made a foreman."

At the end of the move the china was packed: the Reide collection of old Bow and Dresden that stood in those vast reception rooms whose walls were lined with glass-fronted cabinets. The back of each cabinet was formed by a mirror, while the cabinets themselves were most skilfully lighted, and now someone had switched on those hidden lights all down the long side of one of the rooms, so that the lustrous china glowed softly. Form and colour and glaze were there in equal perfection, it seemed to Henry. And seeing perfection his fingers must itch to contact themselves with it, to stroke, to handle. But Riley's were not to be trusted, it appeared. Smith was deeply incensed but powerless for once; Mortlock's had been ordered to pack the china. Yes, but only two men had arrived from Mortlock's, and this was a very extensive collection; moreover, they must work to a specified time, for the china had been lent to an exhibition. They grumbled loudly, shaking their heads.

Henry thought: "If only they'd let me 'elp." And he hovered in their vicinity, too bashful to speak to the experts from Mortlock's.

The next day, much china still remaining unpacked, one of Mortlock's men crushed his thumb
with a hammer. "Can't go on," he announced,
sick and white with the pain, as he groped in his
bag for iodine. "I think I'll take this thumb to a
doctor."

Smith chanced to be passing. "Dear, dear,"
murmured Smith, "what a pity, one might almost
say what a disaster, and the stuff to be got to that
gallery and all." But his voice did not sound in
the least sympathetic.

"You might lend me a man," said the wounded
one's mate, "just until Alf here can report what's
happened."

"I might, but again why should I?" enquired
Smith. "We wasn't thought fit to 'andle this stuff
—not experienced, maybe, just so many kids and
likely to start playing football with it."

"Oh, come off that!" groaned Alf, who was
nursing his thumb.

"Let me, Mr. Smith. Let me 'elp!" exclaimed
Henry.

Smith scowled. "I'll thank you to stop inter-
fering." And then for some reason he changed his
tack. "Oh, all right; I can't spare one of my
seniors. But, mind you, and I say this in front of
a witness, I won't be responsible for what 'appens.

If I'd 'ad charge of the china from the first, I'd
'ave 'ad the right number of expert men; as it is,
I won't be responsible. This young feller 'ere is
quite a newcomer."

He cared not at all what happened to the china,
for Smith was devoid of a sense of beauty, was
moreover as jealous of his prestige as a novelist
or a prima donna, so that now he felt spiteful—let
the kid do his worst. Serve them damned well
right if a piece did get smashed. Yet Smith had a
feeling that this would not occur, for Smith had
been covertly watching Henry, making mental
notes in the interest of the firm.

"Get along with it, Little Tich," he commanded.

Very gently and deftly Henry picked up the
groups with their nymphs and their shepherds and
their egg-brittle foliage. Very gently and deftly
he bound them with paper, then plunged them into
the cases of sawdust. And as he worked he could
feel the smooth glaze giving a sensuous joy to his
hands, while his eyes drank in beauty of colour
and form.

He mused: "Is this the way some fellers feel
when they sees and touches the skin of a woman?
I wonder." But the man from Mortlock's was
speaking.

"Good packing, yours," said the man from

71

Mortlock's. "We're needing a packer—like to make a transfer?"

Henry shook his head. "Not me. 'Tain't enough. I wants more than just this 'ere ancient china . . . though ain't it kind of alive and cool?"

The man grunted. To him it was merely a job, unenlivened by flights of imagination.

Smith strolled past once or twice, elaborately indifferent, but keeping a surreptitious eye upon Henry. "That kid'll shape well, to my mind," ran his thoughts. "Fine sense of balance, and an ox with the heavies . . . gentle as a female with the fragiles . . . safe 'ands . . . he don't fuss but just 'olds them as though 'e meant it."

From that day Henry had no other foreman, for Smith had marked him down for his own, and Smith's jobs, could Henry only have known it, were frequently the most expert at Riley's.

8

For ten years Henry lived at home with his mother. Strange to say, he had never left the mean house that at one time had filled him with something like loathing, never left the street he so much despised or the mother for whom he felt no affection. His sister had married and gone to the Midlands; the ailing Thomas had gone to the churchyard, and his two other brothers were serving abroad, having both developed a taste for the army. Thus it was that Henry and his mother lived alone, she supported in idleness by her son, for quite suddenly Mrs. Dobbs had grown old, much too old to get down and scrub office stairs or, indeed, to attempt any kind of charring.

In the early days of his work at Riley's he had sometimes dreamed of a very different dwelling, of a manor house heavily brooding with oak, and surrounded by trees and old walled gardens; such a house as the wounded Gothic chest of his adolescence might once have dwelt in. But as time went on he dreamed less and less; his work was far too exhausting for dreaming. And then, since the manor was not for him and never could be, why trouble to change? Any home of his must perforce be ugly.

"Can't help the way things is arranged in this world, just got to put up with it," argued Henry.

He earned fairly good money and re-papered the rooms, put in a new sink and painted the woodwork. For the rest he sighed if his shoulders ached in the evenings, was careful to bathe his legs with

cold water before retiring to bed, vaguely wished
that his mother made tastier stews, paid all their
expenses and, when he could afford it, bought
second-hand volumes about antiques, or some
battered piece of old furniture picked up by chance
in a humble sale-room. His manner of speaking
had been somewhat improved by much reading
and frequent contact with the gentry; he now very
seldom ignored an "h"; was, indeed, most particular not to do so. His appearance was neat; he
took pains to be clean, which was no easy task in
his dusty job, but he looked decidedly old for his
age, his thick blue-black hair was already greying.

In his unassuming way he was quite an expert,
and people whom he had moved once or twice and
who knew him would sometimes ask his opinion.
"What do you think of this dole-cupboard, Dobbs?"
or: "I'm doubtful about that Queen Anne bureau—
does it seem right to you?"

Then Henry's rough hand would feel and stroke
very cunningly. "There's a lot to be learnt from
the fingers," he would say. "It's touching that
tells you when a thing's genuine."

With the passing of the years his interests had
narrowed. He still loved all beautifully fashioned
woods, but oak was the wood that he found most
fulfilling; the old, resisting, courageous oak that

taxed the heart and muscles to breaking. Riley's were sometimes employed for repairs, and Henry would watch the steel-hard timber defy and then turn the edge of a tool; and something very deep down in his being, some undreamed of, unrecognised instinct for war, would lift its subconscious head and rejoice at that dumb but valiant revolt against fate, against time, against change and the modern craftsman. Yet together with his love for the stalwart and weighty, there existed a love that was even deeper, the love that he felt for small, fragile things embodying in their fragility all the length and the breadth of an artist's genius. One man may be stirred to protect a fledgeling, another a child, another a woman, but in Henry these delicate treasures of art called forth every gentle and chivalrous instinct, so that he would hold them in his great hands with much tenderness, marvelling to realise how easily his fingers could crush them. Then would come upon Henry the yearning sadness, the humility of soul that encompasses lovers, and when he had shut such an object away and had nailed down the lid of its little deal coffin, he would feel for the moment completely bereaved, so that if one of his mates should speak he would stare at the fellow stupidly; or if he must answer would do so vaguely.

75

9

Everyone respected Henry at Riley's, from old Mr. Riley, the senior partner, down to the most inexperienced fresher. Henry was the type of man people could trust: an honest, sober, untiring workman; a good and reliable citizen. Yet no one was fond of Henry at Riley's. Affection he neither asked for nor gave, and thus he was never accorded affection.

Smith was proud of Henry because he, Smith, had been shown to possess very excellent judgment. "I spotted that chap from the first," he would say; "you can't fool Albert James Smith on a packer." And to Henry: "You'll be 'aving my shoes pretty soon—I'm about played out, as the saying goes. 'Eart, liver, lights and legs all gone. Not much of me left—it's a wearing business."

And he was played out. Played out with the lifting, with the ceaseless strain and wrench on his muscles and on his ageing, labouring heart. He had varicose veins, too, like ropes they were, like knotted discoloured ropes in his calves and his thighs; very terrible indeed to see, for you realised that some day they might burst, and that if this happened it would be good-bye Smith; that Smith who had cased, then lifted and carried, would himself be cased, then lifted and carried . . . As a matter of fact it happened quite soon, and Henry became a foreman.

They were all well content to have Henry as boss, all, that is, except one man, by name Jim Bettridge. Jim Bettridge was Henry's senior by two years and had served the firm for just that much longer. "A weak little pink-eyed rat of a man"; this was how Henry was wont to describe him.

Bettridge had been a failure from birth; he was one of those creatures who seem foredoomed to remain subordinate to their fellows. Promotion would always have passed him by. The new foreman might have been Watts, Wicks or Weston; the one person that he could never have been, as everyone knew very well, was Bettridge.

And then Bettridge was such a cur of a fellow, always cringing and trying to curry favour; always on the alert to secure the first tip; always outwardly smiling but inwardly snarling. And jealous, but jealous of everything; of people's wealth, of their homes, their position; of their silver, their pictures, their furniture; of the very pots and pans in their kitchens. And since jealousy fosters many other distempers, not the least devastating of which is hatred, Jim Bettridge hated all those whose success made him conscious that he would never succeed, and the person he hated most bitterly was Henry. Henry was so strong that the man dared not fight him, dared not even so much as pick a quarrel, and this fact added constant fuel to the flame, until Bettridge could scarcely endure himself; tormented he was by the scourge of his hating. Too timid to become an anarchist, too stupid to become a first-class worker, humble one moment and puffed-up the next, poor but with a great longing for riches, Jim Bettridge was pitied and laughed at by turns. Henry, except when they worked together on a job, completely ignored his existence.

*   *   *   *   *

At about this time Henry decided to marry, and this he did without any emotion. Marriage, he felt, would be good for his health, he supposed that, on the whole, a man needed a woman—at least this was the creed preached by most of his comrades. He was not in love, never had been in love, but he kept his eyes open and one fine day they observed and then rested upon Annie Rogers. She was young, she was buxom, she appeared to be healthy, and she stitched for hours in the carpet department, remodelling carpets for those who had moved; a clumsy, ungrateful task at the best, having nothing of interest or beauty about it.

"Good morning, Miss Rogers."

"Oh . . . good morning, Mr. Dobbs."

"A grand morning."

"Yes . . . oh, yes indeed . . . ain't it lovely!"

Annie was all confusion and pride; to be noticed like this by so splendid a man, by so deeply respected and important a man. She glanced up at Henry then blushed and looked down, running the needle into her thumb from sheer nervousness —the carpet she sewed was one of his orders, Annie remembered.

For two or three weeks Henry spoke to her daily. At the end of a month he made a suggestion: "Would you care to see the Victoria Regyer? It's nice weather for Kew and that plant's a fair wonder. I can take you on Saturday, if you'll come."

His speech sounded to Annie very genteel. " 'E's quite the gentleman . . ." Annie thought. But then of course his speech would be genteel, not like the loose talk she heard from Jim Bettridge.

How she longed to accept, yet she temporised. "Well . . . I don't rightly see as I can . . . there's Jim . . ."

Henry made an expressive sound in his throat.

79

"You two aren't engaged, in a manner of speaking, are you?" he enquired incredulously.

"Not exactly, Mr. Dobbs, but Jim think 'e's my sweet'eart. We walks out together . . . I don't want to 'urt 'im."

"But wouldn't you like to see that water-lily?"

"Oh, I would, Mr. Dobbs."

"Very well, then, it's settled. I'll meet you at the station any time you say, and we'll have a drop of tea together in the gardens."

10

Of course she met him, allured by his strength and the fact that they said he despised all women. And when she had gasped at the sight of the plant and had listened while Henry told her about it, he suggested that they should sit down on the grass, but found a bench on the gravel instead. He was wearing a blue serge suit and dark tie, and she thought him the pattern of manly perfection.

He began: "As you know, I've been made a foreman."

"Oh, I do know, Mr. Dobbs, I do reelly," she faltered.

"I've a nice little house along Fulham way.

There's a new kitchen-sink and all," he continued. "Well, so far I've lived alone with me mother, but mother's getting old, too old for the house-work. Now, a man like me needs a sensible wife—I'm thinking of settling down, as they say." Annie blushed but Henry ignored the blush. "You're a fine healthy girl; never ailing, are you?"

"No, never," breathed Annie.

"Now, that's fine!" he exclaimed. "It's a shame to see you bent double all day, breaking your back over dirty old carpets."

"Oh, Mr. Dobbs . . ."

"Call me Henry—come on!"

"Oh, I can't."

"Yes, you can. We two's going to get married."

She stared at the dogged line of his jaw, immensely attracted yet a little afraid. "But there's Jim . . ." she murmured.

"Jim Bettridge don't count. He's too small to look after a woman," frowned Henry.

"But he did count . . . once . . ."

"Well, he don't any more. That's settled. Now I'm going to give you a kiss."

He glanced round to see that they were un-observed, then he stooped and kissed her stiffly on the lips. "We ought to pull nicely together," he told her.

81

II

When Henry returned from the honeymoon, which had been spent in lodgings at Clacton, Jim Bettridge was waiting for him in the yard. He stepped forward, staring up into Henry's face.

"Congratulations!" he said bitterly.

But Henry was too busy to notice his voice. "Thanks, Bettridge. I'm glad there's no rancour, so to speak."

"Be glad and be damned to you," growled Bettridge.

* * * * *

It was known that Jim Bettridge was taking to drink, that indeed he occasionally drank pretty deeply. "Loved 'er I did," he would whine in his cups, "loved the bitch somethin' awful, Gawd strike me if I didn't. Can't get 'er out of me mind, what's more . . ." And then he would remember the cause of his loss. " 'E thinks 'e's all very fine and large. 'E thinks 'e's a kind of bloody Go-lyer. I'll Go-lyer 'im, I'm just bidin' me time. Didn't 'e snatch Annie out of me arms? I say as 'e did, right out of me arms, and us just on the verge of gettin' married."

He was careful to avoid being drunk during work-hours, very anxious, it seemed, to remain at Riley's; careful also never to cross Henry's bows, for Bettridge could be wily enough when sober. As for Henry, if he thought of Bettridge at all, he did so entirely without remorse. A weak little pink-eyed rat of a man—damned lucky for Annie that she had escaped him. And now it was known that the fellow drank. He had better not turn up drunk on a job, otherwise he would be reported at once, Henry made up his mind to see to that, the prestige of Riley's must be respected.

Meanwhile Annie was running the house in Fulham and appeared, so far, to be most satisfactory. She and old Mrs. Dobbs got on very well and Annie revealed a real talent for cooking. Her health was robust, her temper mild, and she never complained if Henry sat reading instead of taking her out after work.

"I can't abide the Pictures," said Henry. Then perhaps he would summon his wife to his side. "Come here, Annie. Just look at this fine illustration."

Annie would dutifully do as he bade her, staring down at some illustration of oak: an Elizabethan bedstead or chair; a Jacobean cupboard; an ancient credence; or one of those pieces that Henry loved most: a chest splendid because of its Gothic carving. Poor Annie would never know what to say, since to her Henry's fancies appeared very ugly, and her full underlip would begin to sag as it always did when she felt at a loss.

Her husband might glance up impatiently. "Don't like it?"

"N . . . o."

"Prefer Maples, I suppose."

"But, 'Enry, it looks so 'eavy and 'ard."

"Never mind, my girl, get on with the supper."

12

A baby arrived a year after their marriage, to be followed ten months later by another.

"Got a son and a daughter," Henry announced. "Two children's enough, we won't have any more."

Annie would gladly have borne him six, being by inclination a mother, but she acquiesced. " 'Ave it yer own way," she sighed.

"Good girl," smiled Henry, patting her shoulder.

*   *   *   *   *

He never played with his healthy offspring, indeed he seldom accorded them notice. He provided money for food and clothes and a home, and this he considered enough; with the money he gave the matter was ended. He became more and more absorbed in his books, and on every Saturday afternoon he had taken to visiting the museums—South Kensington or the Wallace Collection. He would go by himself, feeling freer to dawdle, to gloat over some early coffer or bibelot, and occasionally he would take copious notes, which he afterwards compared with his books, underlining, or making fresh notes in their margins.

"You're not a man, 'Enry," Annie would tell him, for her temper was now not so sweet as it had been. "You ought to be in one of them glass-fronted cases—seems to me that's reelly about all yer fit for."

Henry would shrug. "I'm not fine enough. Now don't interrupt me, there's a good girl; I believe this chap's gone wrong in a date . . . I can't see how he makes it out Henry VII."

When the baby got whooping-cough Henry was bored and, moreover, he did not trouble to hide it. If the whooping disturbed his peace after work he removed himself and his books from the room. Annie was tired, but he left her to it.

"Can't yer give me an 'and with the child?" she would snap.

But Henry would shake his head. "No—I'm afraid. I dursn't do it, my hands are too strong."

" 'Course not! The poor kid ain't china nor glass. Pity you 'ad any kids, I think; you just oughter 'ave 'ad priceless cups and saucers!"

"Don't be foolish, woman," Henry would warn. "I don't like it."

And Annie would stop being foolish.

Old Mrs. Dobbs from her chair near the fire would peer at her son out of rheumy eyes in which there still lingered a gleam of resentment. "Never was same as other folks—always queer—maybe 'e's a little bit off," she would wheeze. Then conscious of Henry's cold, critical glance. "But 'e's been a good son to me . . . a good son." For old age and long illness had made her timid.

Annie would rock the disconsolate baby, and the baby would whoop until it was sick, at which Henry would turn away in disgust.

"Can't you wipe up that muck?" he would ask angrily. When the baby was sick he could not endure it.

13

The most responsible order that Riley's had so far received came their way about three months later, and it fell to foreman Dobbs and his men. Sir Isaac Epstein was moving his possessions to the country, for Sir Isaac was now very old and his doctors advised him to live out of London.

Sir Isaac arrived one morning in person on the arm of his secretary, Mr. Harris. They remained with the senior partner for an hour, and after their departure Henry was sent for. He found the head of the firm much perturbed.

"You saw that old gentleman, Dobbs?"

"I did, sir."

"And you knew who he was?"

"Yes, Sir Isaac Epstein."

"Quite so; the man whose collections are priceless. You understand? Priceless—beyond all price!"

Henry nodded.

"Well, Dobbs, we're moving his things; we're moving those priceless things down to Surrey. He's done us the honour to trust us, Dobbs. 'No detectives,' he said, 'your firm's reputation is worth all Scotland Yard put together.' He's like that,

I've heard, has faith in mankind. I've heard that he leaves sums of money about just to show the faith he has in his servants. Well, now, listen, please, Dobbs; you're a first-class foreman, but what about your men, will they realise the incalculable value of the stuff they must handle? Weston's excellent, I know, and Briggs is all right . . . then there's Thompson, I believe he packs admirably; I've never heard a complaint of Thompson. But what about the rest?"

"O.K., sir, except one. I'd rather not have Jim Bettridge on this job. I'd prefer not to say more than that, if you please, sir."

"Very good; choose some other man you can trust. I don't mind telling you, Dobbs, I'm worried. I very nearly refused the work, but then I thought of the honour to the firm—I also remembered that I'd got you."

"I'm much obliged for those words, sir," Henry told him.

*　　　*　　　*　　　*　　　*

In due course the Epstein mansion was invaded by Henry Dobbs and his batch of picked workmen. Sir Isaac had been safely got out of the way, and was staying with an unmarried sister at Bournemouth, too feeble these days to supervise the move, which task had been left to Mr. Harris.

The senior partner of Riley's arrived to check over the cases and packing with Henry, whom he introduced as "Our most trusted foreman." Then he hurried back to the depository, for just at that time there was much pressing work and the junior partner was absent through illness.

Mr. Harris was like a hen with its head off, flapping his hands and running round in circles. "Do your men really understand what this means? Most of these things of Sir Isaac's are unique."

Henry did what he could to reassure him.

They began to pack, passing from treasure to treasure. The house was appallingly overcrowded. Priceless works of art stood about on all sides, for Sir Isaac lived cheek by jowl with his collections; that was how he would have them, cheek by jowl, not shut away behind glass in show-cases. In and out of the rooms fussed the nerve-racked Mr. Harris, giving orders to which the men dared not listen. This was no job for an M.A. Oxon. and shortsighted at that, but for Henry Dobbs the expert, the master in his profession.

"Now, sir, it's all right. Don't worry the men. You can trust them; these men know what they're about. Thompson here is one of our tiptop packers."

Mr. Harris wiped beads of sweat from his brow as he tried to control his nerves and his temper. This superior person in the spotless white apron was quietly putting him in his place, was treating him like a tiresome child.

"That's as it may be, but you understand that I am in charge of this move," he retorted.

Very soon Henry's hands seemed everywhere at once, while his competent glance appeared all-seeing. "Easy on, Bill!" "Mind that foliage, mate; them leaves is the most tricky thing about china." "Here, give me that clock, I'll pack him meself, these tortoiseshell clocks are surprisingly fragile."

His fingers caressed each object in turn. "Gawd," he thought, "so much beauty and all in one house, and all belonging to one old man of eighty-three and dying at that. . . . Hard to die and leave so much beauty behind. If Heaven's as fine as they tells us it is, then I wonder why he can't take the lot with him."

He paused for a moment to ease his back and look at his watch—it was nearly twelve; after which he let his eyes roam round the room. His men had just reached Sir Isaac's study, in which he kept all the things he most loved and with which he wished to feel most intimate. It was overcrowded like the rest of the rooms, but more personal, Henry felt, and more friendly. Then Henry suddenly caught his breath, and his bright restless eyes became fixed and staring.

Exquisite it was, that small ivory figure. Exquisite? A clumsy and inadequate word—but then no word was fit to describe it. Words, what were words when it came to such art? Words were born of the flesh, this was born of the soul. . . .

"Makes me want to believe in Gawd," he whispered.

There she stood on a table away in the corner; and she stood alone, nude and chaste and most lovely. Her ivory hands were clasped on her breast, her ivory feet seemed as though arrested in some urgent movement—had it been flight? Nude and chaste and most lovely she stood, all alone, with her ivory face turned to Henry.

"Break off!" he ordered. "It's near dinner-time. You, Thompson, collect everyone that's about, then go to your dinners. I'll do a bit more of the packing—maybe I'll join you later."

Why had he done it? He did not know. He had heard himself giving the order to his men as though in a dream, and now they were gone. He felt frightened. He ran to the door and called.

"Thompson!" he called. "Come back—come back, quick! Come back, I say!" but nobody answered.

He thought: "That little white, fragile thing, so . . . so undefiled. But what's it matter to me? Why did it make me feel kind of queer and shaky the very moment I saw it?"

How quiet the house seemed without the workmen. And where was that blasted fool, Mr. Harris? Oh yes, he remembered, Mr. Harris was out. "I must go to the bank—very urgent business —I won't be gone long." That was what he had said. . . . He had gone to the bank on some urgent business.

Urgent business, all hell! What urgent business? Wasn't it his duty to remain on the spot? How dared he desert such a post of trust? How dared he desert that white, fragile thing? Weren't his master's possessions urgent business? Why, oh, but why had the fool gone out? Yet why not? Why shouldn't Mr. Harris go out? Henry glanced at the statuette over his shoulder. How small it was to express so much, to fill a man's head with preposterous thoughts—it was not much more than seven inches high, he judged . . . yes . . . dangerously small. But wherein lay the danger?

He went to it, lurching a little as he walked;

then he gathered the figure into his hands and laid his cheek against its smooth side. Very gently he rubbed his cheek up and down, sensing the firm and elegant texture. The feel of it gave him a tremulous thrill and he held it out at arm's length for a moment, caressing its loveliness with his eyes. So simple too, its simplicity struck him. He tried to explain this simplicity; no effort on the part of its maker perhaps . . . a thought . . . a swift turning of thought into action, of action into the triumph that he held. And the pose . . . those slim, white, arrested feet . . . surely in another moment they must move . . .

"Why don't you run away from me?" he muttered.

He could feel his heart hammering in his chest. He must have strained his heart, like poor Smith. But he knew very well that he had not strained it. She was nothing unusual, just an ivory figure. But again he knew that he lied to himself. Never before had he seen such perfection of craftsmanship, so delicate yet sure.

"To get the whole spirit into those few inches," he breathed, "amazing! Who done it, I wonder?"

He set down the figure and stared towards the door. Still silence. The house seemed as silent as the grave. Where were the servants? Why didn't they come and make a start at clearing the litter? Curse them, where were they? Why didn't they come? And suddenly Henry wanted to scream, wanted someone near him, someone to clutch. The veins on his temples grew congested and taut. His hand shot out, drew back, stopped halfway and hovered in dreadful uncertainty. Then it closed on the statuette like a trap and crept craftily into his trousers pocket.

14

When the men returned he was sitting on a case staring down at the floor with his hands between his knees.

"I feel sort of off colour," he muttered hoarsely, "giddy like . . . as though I was goin' to vomit." But he motioned them away when they gathered round him. "You all get on with your jobs, and look sharp! This lot must go down to Surrey to-morrow."

Presently he started to wander about, trying to superintend their work but taking no part himself in the packing. Mr. Harris came back and peered in at the door.

"Ah, good; I see that this room's nearly cleared."

"Yes, sir."

"And the library, Dobbs, is that cleared?"

"Not yet, sir. I've just sent some men along."

"I see. At what time do you take this first lot in the morning?"

"As soon as we've loaded the vans from this house—I expect somewhere round about nine. We're ordered to get here sharp by six-thirty. Special job this is, sir, no time to be lost. Mr. Riley knows that we'd work all night if need be. We dursn't take the cases to the warehouse and start off from there—we're afraid of the risk."

"Of course, of course," Mr. Harris agreed. "Well, I'll just go and see what they're doing with the books."

"Certainly, sir, if you wish to," said Henry.

*　　　*　　　*　　　*　　　*

When the men knocked off, Henry made an excuse in order to avoid driving back in their van. "Think I'll just walk a bit—the air'll do me good. No, Bill, I'd rather be alone—you go on. I'm much better; I'll be all right by the morning."

Instinctively he turned into the Park, feeling an urgent need for space. But the Park appeared to

95

have grown very small, it seemed to be closing in upon him. Queer, that. He glanced sharply from side to side. A policeman strolled past.

"Good evening, Bobby. Mild, ain't it?"

"Yes, very."

The policeman passed on.

"Well, I've got some neck!" Henry thought, and he grinned, then decided that he had better stop grinning.

As he walked he began to feel strangely elated, this in spite of the fact that the Park was so cramped. Strangely elated he felt, and young. Daring too—he was bubbling over with daring. The hand in his pocket tightened its grip. He considered himself with a growing interest, surprised to discover how interesting he was, his body, his mind, his soul—if he had one. Absorbingly interesting, Henry Dobbs, born and reared in a poverty amounting to squalor; surrounded by ugliness all his days, yet worshipping beauty—an astonishing chap! Well, now he had beauty, and by Christ, he would keep it!

Married to Annie with a couple of kids. Annie was stupid, her underlip sagged, her teeth were decaying, she was growing too fat. . . . Why had he married her and bred kids? He had never felt the need of a woman. He did not want her—she turned his stomach. In bed he could smell her unwashed, greasy hair and her rancid odour of stale perspiration. Human flesh—why was it so unclean a thing? Annie's flesh was unclean . . . perhaps his was too, though he tried to swill himself down at the sink. And then all the muck of bearing a child and of other things . . . Annie was becoming a slut . . . too intimate by half they had grown, and that was her fault, she was no longer nice, she was quite unashamed . . . it made him heave. Yet she hadn't been beastly when they were first married.

The marvel that lay concealed in his pocket . . . so smooth, so cool, so aloof and so spotless. Never until now had he known what it meant to possess, to be entirely fulfilled by possession.

"I've been needing just this for years," he reflected. "I've been hungry all me life, not knowing for what. Now I do know—I've hungered and thirsted all me life to have something lovely and rare that was mine, something I could cherish because it was mine, something I could touch whenever I wanted . . . touch and look at . . ."

Two lovers passed, walking slowly. The man had his arm around the girl's waist; his eyes were greedy, his face thick and flushed; there were clusters of pimples close to his mouth.

"Fools," muttered Henry unsteadily, "silly fools; a lot they knows about beauty!"

When at last he got home he felt oddly weak.

"What's the matter?" enquired Annie. " 'Ave they given yer the sack?"

"Oh, hold your noise, do!" he retorted roughly.

Without looking at her, he went up to their bedroom. His mind was convulsed by an effort to think. No, he dared not hide it here in this room—Annie was sure to come nosing about. And not in the kitchen. What a hole of a house; you couldn't turn round without being spied on. He stood irresolute, biting his nails and spitting the fragments on to the floor. Wait . . . he had it! The women never went to the loft—too awkward to open the trap from a ladder.

"Annie!" he shouted, "have you swept the loft?"

" 'Course not. Are yer potty? I can't get up since I sprained me ankle, and what's more I'm too busy. If yer wants it swept, then sweep it yerself—or maybe yer'd wish yer old mother to sweep it!"

Bless the woman, did she think she was being sarcastic? He smiled faintly. "No need to lose your shirt, Annie; I was thinking I might as well sweep the place out—give a helping hand, as the saying goes."

"Then yer must be preparin' to meet yer Gawd!"
came Annie's sceptical voice from the kitchen.

He reflected that Annie was now very much
what his mother had been in the days of his childhood: a nagging, uncertain-tempered drab, and he
wondered if Annie's kidney were floating. Then
his thoughts snapped back to the matter in hand.

"Bring me a dust-pan and brush. Look sharp!"

"Oh, all right. What's the fuss?" But Annie
obeyed him.

When she had gone he lighted a candle, fetched
the ladder and clambered through the trap-door.
The loft smelt of mice and the dust of ages.

"This ain't a fit place for you," he sighed, "but
at least I shall have you near me of nights, so that
when I wake up I'll know you're quite close, just
above the bed in which I'll be lying."

15

The next morning the vans drove down into
Surrey, three of them and Henry sat in the fore-
most. His eyes were heavy with sleeplessness. All
through the long night he had lain stark awake,
scheming and then discarding his schemes as being
too risky or utterly worthless. A stupid man now

that this crisis was upon him, yet straining every nerve to be crafty; a naturally honest and law-abiding man, yet striving to grasp the methods of the criminal, and above all a man who was wholly obsessed by a hitherto unsuspected lust—the primitive, combative lust of possession. His thoughts revolved like a squirrel in a cage; round and round they revolved with the wheels of the van, while his brain seemed to throb in time with the engine. But one thought was blindingly, pain-fully clear, so clear that its clarity dimmed every other:

"I've got to keep what I've risked all to get. Don't rightly know how I'm going to act, but I do know one thing—I've got to keep it."

The great lurching vans arrived at the mansion and Henry heard himself issuing orders: "Steady, mates, remember that's porcelain—now carry her steady and lower her gently."

The words came with their accustomed pre-cision; he had said them so often in his career that they sprang automatically to his lips. But he thought: "I'm as cool as a cucumber;" for the sound of his own voice had reassured him. Then he thought: "That bobby . . . the way I spoke up. 'Good evening,' I said; and the thing in me pocket! Now if that wasn't cool!" Then aloud:

"What, Bill? Well, get Thompson to give you a hand if it's heavy."

Mr. Harris was there with innumerable lists. He sucked his pencil and this enraged Henry. He suddenly wanted to tread on the man as a bull-elephant might tread on a wasp, bringing it to a swift, if painful, extinction.

Mr. Harris's voice was precise and cultured. "Everything's to be stacked in the drawing-room, my men; you will find that it is extremely spacious. Are the cases all in? Very good. Are you ready? Then we'll start at once, if you please. First case . . ."

"Containing porcelain," grunted Henry.

*　　　*　　　*　　　*　　　*

For days they continued their methodical labours, now packing in London, now unpacking in Surrey; and every morning Mr. Harris was there in good time to examine each article, to turn it about and about in his hands, to peer at it for hypothetical cracks, or remark upon purely imaginary scratches.

"Ah, a scratch!" he would murmur ominously, making condemnatory notes with his pencil.

To Henry he became unendurable, a constant and ever-increasing torment.

They were checking the collections room by room from the massive, leather-bound inventory-books. How long had they been at this, months or years? Henry would frown as he caught himself wondering. He would take out his watch, observe the time, and forget what time it had been the next second. Seconds and minutes . . . they turned into hours . . . and every hour the horror drew nearer; the horror that had ultimately got to be faced. . . . Yes, and when it leapt on him, it would find him unarmed, a man who had no idea what he would do, or what he would say, a man without plans. "Gently, Alf, with that casket, she's rock-crystal." Even in this his extremity he must care for the things that had brought romance to an otherwise drab and ugly existence.

Dining-room. Library. When would it come? Drawing-room; not for a long while, it seemed, that drawing-room in London had been stacked with possessions. Smoking-room. Did Mr. Harris know something? Was he having a game like a cat with a mouse? Why had he told them not to uncase the things from the study until he so ordered? He had said: "Leave the study cases alone until I tell you to open them, please. I must give those cases my whole attention." A true bill? Or did he perhaps suspect, and suspecting had he

decided to torture? Henry Dobbs, pull yourself
together, my man, you're not really scared . . . of
course he knows nothing! But when would it
come? This waiting was grotesque, preposterous.
And when it did come, what then? The sweat
would break out on Henry's brow and trickle
unheeded into his eyes, until in the end he must
brush them with his hand.

"Warm work . . ." he would mumble, by way
of explanation.

"Ball-room."

How slowly that pompous ass spoke, chewing
the cud of every item, leaving no smallest detail
unread. Did he think that they wanted a lecture
on art? But perhaps it was he who had made those
lists, so precise, so damnably clear and precise.

"And now the study, Dobbs. Are you ready?"

For a moment the room spun round and went
black; then Henry heard his own voice, strong and
calm: "Yes, sir. The cases are just over there. I
believe you'll find the whole lot of 'em together."
And to Thompson: "You and Bill must uncase
this lot, and go softly, mind, with your hammer
and chisel."

"Shall I clear a space?" Thompson enquired,
looking up.

"Of course; better clear those refectory tables."

When at last the things were in readiness, Mr. Harris started reading even more slowly. He now seemed to be savouring every word as a connoisseur will savour old port—drinking in sips, pausing over each mouthful.

"Man and horse in armour (Prentice piece)," he intoned. "Virgin and Child by Andrea Della Robbia (Florentine School, 1466) . . . Limoges Enamel Dish: the Birth of Venus by Penicaud III. (Late XVI century) . . . Chalice of Enamelled Glass (XVI century). Probably by a Venetian workman . . . Mug of Rock-Crystal mounted in Gold. Signed: H.B. Dated 1765; and having a small chip out of the handle . . . Head of Bishop's Crozier in Silver-Gilt set with cabochon emeralds, sapphires and rubies. French workmanship (XIV century) . . . Gold Incense Boat in the form of a Galley (XVII century. Spanish or Italian) . . . Boxwood Tabernacle elaborately carved with stories from the Gospels (about 1504, or might be somewhat earlier. Flemish) . . . Wax Relief of the Annunciation. Artist unknown (later XVI century). Probably South German . . . Pair of Candlesticks, Lapis Lazuli and Gilt, with Cupids at base (Early Louis XV)." He ticked off the articles one by one in his leather-bound tome, as Henry found them.

Then: "Ivory Statuette of Nude Female Figure; attributed to Leonardo da Vinci."

No one spoke.

Mr. Harris looked up in surprise: "What's the matter?" he demanded.

But still no one spoke.

Mr. Harris turned the colour of putty.

With his neck thrust forward he peered round the room. "Where's that ivory statuette?" he said loudly.

The men looked at Henry and then at each other.

"I never saw it."

"Don't think I did, either."

"I've a kind of recollection . . . leastways I didn't pack it."

Their faces were stupid, puzzled and distressed.

Henry said: "If that figure was there, then it's here. Where else could it be, sir? We're bound to find it."

"You say, '*If* it was there,' but, good God, man, I saw it! I myself put it out on a table to be cased. It was in the far corner of Sir Isaac's study."

"As I said, if that ivory figure was there, then it must be here, sir," Henry repeated.

He felt amazingly cool and detached, much as though this affair in no way concerned him. He could almost have smiled at the sudden collapse of Mr. Harris, who had flung down his book and was showing every symptom of panic. Plunging his shaking hands into the shavings, he proceeded to hurl them about the room.

"If you'll allow us to go through that packing, it will be more in order, sir," Henry told him.

"Oh, my God!" Mr. Harris sounded very near tears. "What will Sir Isaac say? This will kill him! Leonardo da Vinci . . . priceless, unique! Leonardo da Vinci, the only example . . . and I put it on that table myself . . . I know the precise spot on which I stood it!"

He was running about like a creature possessed. In the end they all were, they had caught the infection, all, that is, except Henry, whose voice remained chill. "Now then, steady, please. Thompson, look through this litter. And you, Bill, go with Weston and search the empties."

But the men, terrified, had got out of hand; in their fear they completely ignored their foreman. Upstairs and down like a pack of mad hounds; shouting to each other like hounds giving tongue, their voices sounding shrill and unnatural.

Henry scowled as he followed close on their heels. "This ain't no way to conduct yourselves. Stop scampering and bawling all over the house and do as I orders, if you please. First those empties outside." But no one obeyed him.

After more than three hours of the fruitless hunt a dangerous calm came upon Mr. Harris. They heard him calling up Scotland Yard, heard him offering two thousand pounds reward, and when he returned he eyed the men coldly.

"You will all rest under the gravest suspicion until this thing is forthcoming," he told them. "I shall now telephone to Sir Isaac Epstein, then return to Riley's depository with you. None of the servants will leave the house. Everything is out of the vans, I understand, and that being so you will kindly touch nothing. The rooms must be left precisely as they are to assist the police in making their inspection. Now then, my good man, keep your hands off that case. Did you hear my orders? You did? Then obey them!"

In a deathly silence the men drove back, preceded by Mr. Harris in his motor. Arrived at Riley's, he got out of his car and was shown into old Mr. Riley's office. Meanwhile the men hung about in groups, still silent. Their faces looked scared and dejected.

Henry said: "Stop acting like a lot of pickpockets. You ain't pinched the thing, have you, so what's the trouble? It's my opinion it was never put out. I'll bet you they find it in some cupboard or drawer. The place to look for it's the London house, mark my words." At that moment Henry was sent for.

Mr. Riley senior was sitting at his desk.

"Gawd Almighty, he's gone suddenly crumpled," thought Henry.

Then Mr. Riley senior looked up and spoke: "Dobbs, did you see this statuette?"

Henry met his eye squarely. "No, sir, I didn't."

"But I say that you must have!" Mr. Harris exclaimed.

Henry ignored this, and addressed his employer: "Excuse me, sir, but the house here in London has not been searched yet. Now it seems to me . . ."

Mr. Riley held up an unsteady hand. "The police have already been there and found nothing." Then he turned to Mr. Harris. "This is Friday, sir; the loss was discovered in Surrey this morning. Now, when did you last see the statuette?"

Mr. Harris considered, clearing his throat. "On a Sunday evening, twelve days ago. I went into the study and collected some things for the men to pack when they came the next morning. I took the statuette out of its case and carefully dusted it with my own hands; then I stood it on a table in the corner. There was nothing on that table but the statuette."

"And had it a plinth of any kind?"

"No. It stood on a small piece of ivory—the base was one with the figure itself."

"I see. It would therefore be easily concealed?"

"Very easily indeed, the whole thing was so small, rather less than seven inches in height, it measured."

Mr. Riley considered. "And you saw it on Sunday. Did you see it again on the Monday morning?"

"I did not . . . I really don't think that I can have. I was called out on business during that morning, and when I returned they were working in the study, but I did not go right into the room. I remember I went on to the library. You see, I found the study in charge of your foreman."

"And on Monday evening, sir?"

"On Monday evening I did go in after the men had left. All the cases had been packed and were ready to start. I naturally thought that the statuette had been cased and would therefore arrive with the rest. What else was I to think if your men are trustworthy?"

"Had you pointed the statuette out to Dobbs?"

"No, I cannot remember having done so. But

I'd told him that everything in that room, in Sir Isaac's study, was of immense value."

"Yet you did not check over the inventory with him before packing?"

"Of course not—once was surely enough. I decided to leave it until they unpacked."

"I think that was a pity," remarked Mr. Riley. Then he said: "Well, now, sir, you saw it on Sunday when you took it from its case and placed it on a table. But you did not see it on Monday, you say. Sir Isaac's servants were in the house; they slept in the house on that Sunday night, which my men did not do. I'm accusing no one, but have you thought of theft by some member of the staff—or even, perhaps, by some outside person? A burglar may have got access to the room."

"The latter is impossible, I should think; I'm told that the fastenings were all intact."

"Well, then, mayn't the statuette have been taken from the house by some inmate during the night?"

Mr. Harris looked shocked. "Sir Isaac's servants have been with him for many years," he protested.

"As my men have with me," Mr. Riley replied. "Dobbs, how long is it now since you came to this firm?"

"Going on for eleven years," muttered Henry.

The men were now sent for and searchingly questioned in the presence of Mr. Harris and their foreman. They grew confused. There were so many things. They had seen one or two little ivory figures . . . or had they been silver? Or had they been bronze or porcelain or gilt? There were so many things. Only Thompson thought that he might have noticed the missing statuette, but he was not sure; the corners of Sir Isaac's study were dark, the whole room was on the dark side, he declared. No, on second thoughts, he felt sure he had not seen it.

Mr. Riley sighed. "You may go," he told them, "and you, Dobbs, can go too." Then he turned to Mr. Harris. "I wish to see someone from Scotland Yard. You say that you have asked an inspector to call?"

"He should be here now," rejoined Mr. Harris.

16

The warehouse hummed all day long with the news. Men went about their duties with very grave faces. Everyone felt this disgrace to the firm, everyone pitied the senior partner—he had been a just man and was liked and respected. Only Bettridge appeared to take the thing lightly; when told, he had whistled and raised his eyebrows. But he turned very friendly to all the men who were under this hateful cloud of suspicion, and especially friendly to Henry, he turned.

"Wonder why that little pink-eyed rat of a man wants to come sucking up to me?" pondered Henry.

People from Scotland Yard came and went. It was whispered that Mr. Harris was suspected. Had he not been the last to see the damn thing? And who better than he knew the statuette's value? Sir Isaac's old servants came in for their share of the sordid business; but Henry, as the foreman who had actually been in charge of the move, was questioned and re-questioned again and again. There had been that hour when the others were at dinner and he had remained alone in the study. Why had he not gone to dinner with the rest? They always seemed to be asking him this; he would dread it like a recurrent nightmare. Yet his answers never faltered nor failed. " 'Cause I felt rather queer." And this was borne out by the men who had come back to find him ill.

"Why didn't you tell the men you felt ill before they left?"

" 'Cause I didn't want to scare them. I didn't want to take their minds off their job—I knew that some of the things were priceless."

"Particularly that small statuette. You knew that was priceless, of course. Come now, Dobbs."

"As I didn't even know that the thing existed, how could I know it was priceless, sir?"

"But it stood on a table in a corner of the room, yet you ask me to believe that you didn't see it? Remember it was white and would show up well."

"That's so, sir. I've been told it was ivory. But I can't meself credit that it was where you say; if it had been, why, surely I must have seen it."

Always the same soul-sickening questions, put differently sometimes in order to trap him, now as harsh and abrupt as the lash of a whip, now as soft and conciliatory as satin. And his rather slow mind, dulled by years of toil, straining like a tired overloaded horse—straining horribly, but so far not failing.

Sir Isaac came back to London from Bournemouth, much against the advice of his eminent doctors. He was wounded to the depths of his collector's soul by the loss of the Leonardo da Vinci. He doubled the reward—four thousand pounds now! Then he cursed the police for incompetence and employed a firm of private detectives.

Whole columns began to appear in the papers regarding the theft of the priceless art treasure: its history, not always quite accurately told; its description, not always felicitously worded.

Henry read one of these journalistic efforts, and was filled with a secret, impotent fury. "What a way to describe such a thing," he raged; "but then they haven't seen it and won't—leastways, if I can prevent 'em they won't. How much would they understand if they did? Why, nothing. The idea of calling her 'dainty.' "

There were times now when he was seized with sheer panic, when he had some ado to master his nerves, which were playing him disconcerting tricks, not only at home but at the warehouse. Riley's was under a heavy cloud, and until it was lifted the senior partner must tread warily in his dealings with clients. He believed in the innocence of his men and would not dismiss them; nevertheless he dared not employ them on specialist jobs. The whole business had caused such publicity, and Henry's name had appeared in the papers together with a mysterious snapshot. Thus it was that the men had little to do and must hang about giving a hand where they could; sweeping the yard or the warehouse floors, stacking empty cases or collecting packing. And thus it was that Henry, unoccupied save by tasks that required no concentration, concentrated more and more on himself, and on his daily increasing terror.

He would think that everyone eyed him askance, that he was a topic of constant discussion, that voices dropped meaningly at his approach, that his mates looked on him with hostile suspicion.

He would think he heard footsteps in quiet streets; sly, terrible footsteps that always followed; and his scalp would tingle, his hands grow moist as he dodged down this alleyway and then that, in an effort to shake off those following footsteps. But when at last he could bear it no longer and must jerk himself round to confront his pursuer, fists clenched, lips drawn starkly back from his teeth, he would find that he was confronted by nothing. Then shaking his head, he would chide himself:

"Don't be such a bloody fool, Henry Dobbs. You're behaving as though you thought they could hang you."

He began to frequent socialistic meetings. He who had hitherto voted Tory now began to listen with all his ears to the doctrines expounded by eager young men who believed every word that they said—or almost. But though he was told that the useless rich should be speedily swept from the face of the earth in order that the poor might acquire their possessions, and though this must mean that he, Henry Dobbs, had an obvious right to the thing he had stolen, he remained unconvinced.

"Gawd Almighty," he thought, "I didn't take it because I'd the right; I took it because I needed it so, because I'd been needing it most of me life, ever since I was just a great lumbering kid and used to stand staring into those windows."

He grew bored with the meetings, and moreover they shocked him. What a way to speak of Sir Isaac Epstein; to call him a vampire, a parasite, merely because he had been born wealthy. To demand that his riches be confiscated by the State— what would happen to his collections? So much loveliness thrown to an ignorant mob; spat upon, trampled down by the mob.

"I'd rather give it him back, yes, I would. I'd rather he had it a thousand times . . . but I mean to keep it meself," mused Henry.

His moods were as variable as the wind; from panic he would veer to self-confidence, to a self-confidence that made him feel reckless. He would want to laugh in the teeth of the world; would itch to tell Annie the astounding truth just for the pleasure of watching her face and hearing her cry of dismay and horror.

She would almost certainly run to his mother. "Our 'Enry's a thief! Oh, what'll we do? There's the children and all . . . oh, what'll we do?"

And his mother would wag her palsied head: "I always suspected that boy was a dark 'un." Just this and nothing more she would say; content with the knowledge that she had been right, content to be justified in her dislike of the son who was feeding and clothing her carcass.

But through all these changing and desperate moods there was something unchanging, something essential; the longing to see, the longing to touch, the longing to contact his being with beauty. And he dared not see, and he dared not touch, which but served to intensify this longing. He was never alone in the box of a house, someone always seemed to be at his elbow; a child ready to question or to exclaim; his wife ready to nag—perhaps even his mother. Should they chance to go out, they always came in, it was cause and effect—go out, come in. No peace and no privacy anywhere.

"Maybe I'll cut and run," he would think; "maybe I'll cut and run, taking it with me."

Upstairs, and then through the creaking trap-door, that was the way. And once in the loft . . . the heap of old boxes against the wall . . . under the lid of the seventh box, counting from the top—

that was how he had piled them. To see, to touch, just once, only once. Lord, how his hands sometimes ached for the thing, for its exquisite shape, its smoothness, its coolness.

He thrust back the impulse. "Mad, that's what I am. Let the row blow over a bit, anyway. They'll get tired of their yapping after a while, they'll be bound to—can't go on yapping for ever."

But he could not rest. To see—to touch. It was like the craving for food and drink; a craving of the body but also of the mind, since the need stimulated imagination. It was stronger even than the impulse to steal—that, he told himself now, he might have resisted. But once having made the temptation his own, he could scarcely endure this curb on his passion. To see, to touch, just once— only once. No lover could have longed more consumedly for a contact denied him by harsh separation.

*   *   *   *   *

His repugnance to Annie was fast turning to hatred; she was terribly active in spite of her fat and that treacherous ankle—oh, but terribly active. He could never creep upstairs but Annie must follow, never look at the trap-door but Annie must catch him, and catching him, show curiosity. "Is anything wrong? What yer gapin' at, 'Enry?"

And surely her eyes had grown watchful of late, sly and watchful as though there were something to watch, some secret that she might discover by watching? And her voice when she caught him near that trap-door—surely her voice was full of suspicion? It was happening every day now, this spying, so hard to endure, so hard to evade, and the thought of it filled him with brooding anger. His mother he found less intolerable—she was partially crippled by rheumatism. But Annie, ah, there was a woman to fear, a woman who would scream and give you away, unless . . . His thoughts would start back with a jerk; then pale to the lips he would stand staring at her.

"Stop yer starin' at me!" Annie might exclaim, and her voice would hold in it a shrill note of fear, and hearing that note of fear in her voice, he would have to clench his big hands, lest he strike her.

Mad, but of course he was going mad. He, such a quiet and peaceable man, to be thinking these horrible, bestial thoughts, to be wanting to squeeze Annie's thick red throat—Annie, who had used to sit stitching for hours with that hard, detestable carpet thread . . . And one evening he remembered his courtship of Annie.

"It's a shame to see you bent double all day,

breaking your back over dirty old carpets."

"Oh, Mr. Dobbs . . ."

"Call me Henry . . . Come on!"

How young she had been, how shy and respectful. Not bad-looking either, with her pink and
white skin. . . . Neat too—she had been very
clean and neat. And her voice had been gentle
because she was shy, whereas now it was constantly
raucous with nagging. Queer, the change in
Annie . . . how had it happened? He had done
his best for her by earning good money. . . . He
was sober; she could not accuse him of drink nor
could she accuse him of going with whores. He
frowned, struck a match, and lighted his pipe.

"Annie," he said, "have you been happy with
me?"

It was her turn to stare. "What yer gettin' at?"

"Nothing," he muttered. "Why don't you go
out for a bit?" If only she would go out!

But she shook her head. "No, I've got sewin' to
do; that Syd's gettin' awful 'ard on 'is clothes, and
yer none too easy yerself on yer vests."

He sighed. He had fully expected some such
answer.

*　　　*　　　*　　　*　　　*

It was now that a very surprising thing happened: Jim Bettridge walked in one Saturday evening.

"Well, Annie," he said, holding out his hand; "well, Dobbs, I 'ope you won't take this amiss, but seein' as 'ow I'm a lonely chap I thought as perhaps I might come along. . . . I've been tryin' me best to keep off the drink and it 'elps me to be with a man that's so steady. But of course if you're thinkin' as I'm in the way . . ."

What could they do but make him feel welcome?

He stayed on to supper, and after the meal he made himself pleasant to Henry's mother, moving her chair and finding her shawl. Indeed he appeared most anxious to please—very humble, he seemed; very grateful, he seemed.

"Means more than you knows to me, this sort of thing," he told Henry, when he finally took his departure.

And apparently it did, for he came pretty often, constantly turning up uninvited.

"I don't trust 'im. What's 'e 'opin' to get out of us?" frowned Annie; "we ain't The Crusade of Rescue! 'Owever I could 'ave fancied that feller I don't know; 'e makes me creep, 'e's so slimy."

Henry said: "Perhaps he is trying to keep straight; it may be that." But he did not believe it. He was thinking: "She's right; I don't trust him either. What's it mean, his hanging around this house? For more than ten years we've worked side by side, and in all that time he's never come near us. 'Cause why? 'Cause we ain't been on those sort of terms. I don't trust him and, moreover, I don't care for his eyes—don't seem able to look me straight in the face. And why is he always nosing about, offering to help wash plates in the scullery, offering to go and fetch things from upstairs? 'Tain't natural, leastways in a chap like Bettridge."

But natural or not, Bettridge now haunted Henry, for it seemed that Bettridge had some business in Fulham, so that they would constantly meet in the streets. And once Henry fancied that Bettridge was standing at the corner, intently watching the house. It was dusk, and when Henry called no one replied. The figure turned and walked quickly away. Impossible to tell in the uncertain light of late afternoon, impossible to tell—perhaps it was some other mean-looking chap. But all that evening Henry felt jumpy. Nor could he get rid of Bettridge at Riley's, for whenever the fellow was not on a job he would make it his business to keep very close, and when Henry went out to his dinner at twelve, at the very next table to his would be Bettridge.

Yes, and now Bettridge always wanted to talk about the theft at Sir Isaac Epstein's. "Terrible thing for the firm," he would say; "what do you make of that business, Dobbs? In your opinion, 'ow did it 'appen? You was there in the study all the time—didn't even go out for a snack of food. 'Oo done it, do yer think, that secretary blighter? Or was it, maybe, one of the servants? Any'ow, it's a terrible thing for the firm." And then he would put his head on one side and wait until Henry contrived an answer.

Detestable it was, yet there seemed no escape, for Bettridge blandly refused to quarrel. "Go on, curse me up and down 'ill if yer wants; if I can't stand that much from an old friend like you, then there must be somethin' the matter with me. Any'ow, I don't wonder yer feels a bit cheap; in your shoes I'd be drinkin' meself to death—I would that—and you a foreman and all! Thank the Lord yer wouldn't have me on that job; now if I'd been along yer'd have thought as I'd done it."

Danger. Hemmed in upon every side. The whole world composed of inquisitive eyes, of voices asking inquisitive questions; of mysterious figures watching the house, of people who turned to stare in the streets. And when you got home from it all, dead-beat, no privacy, nowhere to hide from eyes, nowhere to sit down and think the thing out—not a corner, not a hole or corner in the place that was safe from the ceaseless spying of Annie.

17

For two months the hue and cry continued, after that it began to die down a little. Sir Isaac Epstein returned to Bournemouth a very sick man—he was broken-hearted. A watch was kept on his house in London and also on his mansion in Surrey. Scotland Yard, it was said, had the matter in hand, but not, so far, the Leonardo da Vinci.

It was April now, and the spirit of spring had come all of a sudden, bewitching the city. Henry walked home from the warehouse one evening in a dazzle of rainy luminous sunset, and his eyes perceived the beauty of the streets; they seemed changed by that queer, unearthly light.

"I'm not much of a one for nature," he mused, "but I must say this sunset is something extra."

The gleam of the pavements made him slightly giddy. He did not find the sensation unpleasant. Moreover, he seemed to be walking on air, and this also was not an unpleasant sensation. He felt

happy and brave. Brave because he was happy—or
was it the other way round? He wondered. No
matter, it did not matter at all. Nothing mattered
but what he was going to do. . . .

"To-night," he said softly under his breath,
"to-night—just after the lamps are lighted."

He was kind, unusually kind to Annie. When he
got home he stooped and kissed her. "I've brought
you some sweets for the kids," he announced;
"pear-drops, because you likes them as well."

She flushed. "Just fancy your rememberin'
that!" and putting a pear-drop into her mouth she
sucked it.

Henry looked away quickly.

At supper he tried to swallow, but could not.

"Nothin' wrong with yer, is there?" Annie
asked him.

" 'Course there isn't; I'm only feeling a bit
slack . . . it's this heat. It's uncommonly warm
for April." He glanced at the clock, and suddenly:
"Listen! What's that funny scraping noise over-
head? Don't you hear it? A kind of scraping
noise."

"Not burglars, 'Enry . . ." his mother began.

"Well now, I don't know—think I'll just take
a peep. You two stop quietly here with the kids.
No need to be scared, just stop quietly here." He

looked round for a weapon and grasped the poker.

They heard him go clumping up the stairs. Then his voice: "Gawd 'elp yer, young feller-me-lad!" Then another sound—the trap-door on the landing. Then more threats: "Now, matey, take care of yourself—there won't be a great lot left if I catch yer!"

In less than five minutes he had come down again. "Not so much as the skin of a louse," he told them. Presently he said: "Think I'll go for a turn—it's that fine. I don't suppose I'll be late, but in any case neither of you's to wait up; Annie's looking dead-beat. Now mind what I say, I expect to come home and find you both snoring."

*   *   *   *   *

Once outside the house he began to laugh softly. "Poor Annie . . . poor ugly, pitiful slut. Can't help feeling kind of sorry to-night. . . . But Lord, I was cute; I took her in proper!"

He was walking quickly towards the Park. An exquisite hardness lay against his breast, he placed his hand over it, holding it closer.

He turned into the Park at Alexandra Gate. How quiet it was, how mercifully lonely. And that exquisite hardness against his breast—the sense of security in possession. No one to question him, no one to spy. It was growing late, the Park was deserted—that was good, very good, but he mustn't waste time—they'd be closing the Park gates at twelve o'clock; besides, someone might pass at any moment.

He stepped over the palings not far from the bridge and stood motionless on the grass for a minute. He listened. Not a sound except his own heart.

"Be quiet now," he whispered, "not so much of yer beating!"

There were stars and a small inadequate moon, but light enough from a lamp near by. He lurched towards it, tore open his clothes and clutched at the thing that lay against his skin; then he drew it forth, supremely exultant. His hands were shaking, his breath came in sobs. He was like a man who has run a great race and who holds the laurels of victory before falling. And he seemed to be beseeching the thing with his eyes—praying to it with his bloodshot, adoring eyes. The little white ivory statuette lay chastely upon his work-stained palm—immaculate, enduring but unresponsive.

"'Allo, Dobbs!" Jim Bettridge's voice, and quite close. "Star-gazin'? Well, now, it's a priceless night—never enjoyed a night more in me life—sweet it is with all them stars and that moon . . ."

Henry's hand swooped into the pocket of his coat. "What the hell are you doing out here?" he gasped. Then he spat to show his complete indifference.

Bettridge grinned. "Same as you; leastwise I suppose so . . . just fillin' me lungs with oxygen. Isn't that what you've been doin', matey?"

For one moment Henry thought he must strike, must strike down and then obliterate this man with the crafty, smirking, insolent face; but the impulse passed, leaving him badly shaken. He tried to collect his reeling wits, tried to gauge the full extent of his peril. But perhaps he was not in peril after all. Had Jim Bettridge seen? It was very unlikely. Just a small patch of lamplight and then those trees. . . . No one could be certain of a thing under trees. . . . In any case Bettridge was probably half drunk . . .

"I'm going home," Henry told him briefly.

Bettridge was close to his elbow now. "Same here," he remarked. "I'll walk along with you."

"Don't trouble—my house will be out of your way."

"What about it? I'll enjoy the stroll," smiled

Bettridge. In silence they turned towards the gate, then Bettridge began to speak very softly; "Lovely, them stars—don't yer think so, mate? Lord, 'ow the stars do take a man back . . . you and me's not quite so young as we was . . . no, not by a long way."

Henry ignored him.

Bettridge went on talking; his voice sounded dreamy. "Lord, Lord, we've been through some times, ain't we, Dobbs? What with Annie and all . . . Lord, I loved that girl! You done me the dirty over that, Dobbs, and you can't say no— you was bloody dirty. But I ain't retaliated—not yet—must be a kind of dummy or somethin', me lovin' Annie the way I did. It's not many chaps would 'ave took it lyin' down, but then that's me: I can't 'arbour malice. Queer 'ow you managed to get all the plums . . . Annie and foreman, me wantin' both. Felt I'd a right to 'em, too, you understand . . . Damned queer 'ow you've managed to do me down, ain't it?"

What was it saying, that infuriating voice, drivelling on and on about Annie. A senseless, disgusting, maudlin voice with an undertone of something else in it. Yes, but what? Henry's mouth went suddenly dry. Was it an undertone of hatred?

They had reached Exhibition Road by now and were walking towards South Kensington Station. Bettridge had taken Henry's arm.

"I'm that full of rememberin', to-night," he drawled; "crikey, but I'm full to the neck of rememberin'."

Presently they had passed the station, and turning down Pelham Street, had reached Fulham Road. The road looked deserted; it had started to rain. The solitary policeman on point-duty shook his cape, and Bettridge's grip on Henry's arm tightened.

Bettridge said: "Let's cross 'ere—I'm nervous of traffic. Oh, but straight I am—let's cross 'ere by the bobby."

Nervous of traffic? What the hell did he mean? There was no traffic at this time of night . . . And why that ridiculous clinging hand? "Let go of my arm. What yer getting at?" But the fingers still clung.

"Nothin'. Ain't you jumpy! Come on, that bobby 'll see us across. It's Gawd's truth as I'm nervous of motors these days, the way they comes swoopin' and hootin' round corners."

They had come abreast of the policeman by now. He yawned and glanced at them casually. Then Bettridge's free hand was grasping his sleeve.

"Officer, arrest this 'ere man, 'e's a thief! Ever 'eard of the Vinci statuette? Well, 'e's got it!"

Henry stood motionless as though turned to stone; all power of movement seemed to have left him.

"Now, don't come none of yer jokes over me, I'm not for it," snapped the incredulous policeman.

And still Henry stood there, dumb, stupefied; his great strength held back like a hound in leash by his staggering wits that refused to release it.

"If yer such a fool as not to believe me, then look in the right-'and pocket of 'is coat. Quick, quick! Oh, for Gawd's sake be quick!" screamed Bettridge.

The policeman swung round and seized Henry's collar, while Bettridge still clung to his arm like a limpet. Then Henry made a queer sound in his throat and abruptly woke up—a terrific awakening.

Even as the muscles of Samson swelled to destroy the Philistines in their temple, so now Henry's muscles tightened and swelled to destroy his puny antagonists. Bettridge fell back with a shriek of pain—his arm had snapped in two like a pipe-stem. Blood was trickling into the constable's eyes and he failed to get his whistle to his lips. But he would not let go; he was wiry and young, and besides, this arrest might bring him promotion. Backwards and forwards they swayed.

"Help!" yelled Bettridge, "help! help! there's a thief 'ere what's murderin' a policeman!"

Then quite suddenly Henry was standing stock-still. "It's O.K., Bobby—that swine's right, I've got it. It's here, as he says, in the pocket of me coat. I'll come quiet . . . Don't let's rough-house any more. . . . Chances are if we goes on like this we'll harm it."

18

It was four years, and for a first offence. But the judge had been shocked by the whole affair. Henry had held a position of trust and, moreover, when arrested he had shown great violence. Above all the judge was a connoisseur of art, and the theft had concerned a Leonardo da Vinci.

After the sentence they led Henry away, but all through that gruelling trial he had seen it. They had placed it upon a table in the court for the callous, inquisitive crowd to gape at—the lovely, innocent, patient thing. So helpless and shamed it had looked to Henry. He had cried out hoarsely; they had thought it was fear and had told him, kindly enough, to be silent. In the end he had

scarcely raised his eyes, and this they had thought
was humiliation.

*   *   *   *   *

They let Annie come to him to say good-bye—
he had not expressed a desire to see her. She found
him huddled in a corner of his cell, and finding him
thus her thoughts slipped back so that she became
young and gentle again, and the mother-instinct
leapt up in her heart, for to her he seemed like an
unhappy child much in need of pity and
consolation.

" 'Enry . . ."

"Yes, Annie?"

"Oh, 'Enry . . . my dear."

He glanced at her. "Stop being foolish,
woman."

"But, 'Enry, yer cryin' . . . oh, 'Enry, *don't!*
Me and the children will be all right, I promise yer
we will; don't go frettin' like this . . . and when
yer gets out we'll be waitin' for yer."

"Gawd!" he choked, "it ain't that . . . but you
can't understand . . . no, of course you can't
understand; how could you? But . . . oh, Gawd
. . . I'll never see it again . . ."

She stared at him, bewildered, abashed. Her
untidy hat had slipped backward and sideways, her

face was a blank, her underlip sagged.

"Me and the children . . ." she began, then stopped; smitten dumb by a glimmer of understanding.

Presently he rubbed his eyes with his sleeve, and when next he spoke he did so calmly: "Four years," he said in a thoughtful voice, "four years . . . I should think he gave me pretty well the limit. Four years is a long time to live in a jail, seeing bars and blank walls and ugliness, a long time. . . . But mind you, Annie, it was worth it!"

FRÄULEIN SCHWARTZ

M<small>RS.</small> R<small>AYMOND</small> preferred that her
boarding-house should be known as a private
family hotel, thus: "Raymond's Private Hotel" had
been painted in brown on the peeling Corinthian
columns, and again above the shabby front door
in gilt letters across the fanlight. The house stood
in a street that had seen better days; it was one of
those endless Pimlico streets that meander dully
towards the river. All its houses were fashioned
precisely alike: tall fronts, sash windows, damp
areas; moreover, they were large but without
dignity, and solid while conveying no sense of
comfort.

Mrs. Raymond was the childless widow of
a merchant who had had the misfortune to
speculate in rubber; of that rash speculation
nothing now remained but a starved rubber
plant in the dining-room window. However,
being a hard-headed woman and blessed by a lack
of imagination, she had promptly opened a
boarding-house which pretended to offer every
home comfort.

"A home from home," Mrs. Raymond would say, "that's what I aim at—a home from home." And since it was cheap as such places went, her clients preferred not to contradict her.

Like every experienced landlady, Mrs. Raymond had a very marked preference in boarders. She much preferred youthful and unattached men because, as a rule, they were docile and timid. At this time she had three such young men in her house: Mr. Pitt, Mr. Narayan Dutt and Mr. Winter.

Mr. Pitt belonged to the Y.M.C.A. He was secretary of some local branch, and he made a hobby of physical training. Mr. Pitt spent much time running round Richmond Park in modest duck shorts and a drenched cotton singlet. When he ran his hands sawed the air helplessly, his chest heaved and his eyes bulged behind his glasses. Mr. Narayan Dutt, who hailed from Bengal, was an earnest and a diligent medical student; he affected amazingly tight grey clothes and soft boots of a very unusual yellow. Mr. Winter worked in a city office; his prospects were poor and so was his health—he suffered from chronic nervous dyspepsia.

Apart from a few occasional boarders, there were four other "regulars," as they were called: Colonel Armstrong, of doubtful antecedents—he was said to be late of the Volunteers—two spinster sisters, the Misses Trevelyan, whose father had been a naval paymaster and who therefore despised the ambiguous Colonel, and an elderly person, by name Fräulein Schwartz, who gave German lessons at a couple of schools and eked out a living with private pupils.

Fräulein Schwartz was little and round and fifty, with neat greying hair and a very high bosom. She frequently sighed, and whenever this happened the plaid silk of her blouse creaked in sympathy—like many a German of her generation she displayed a mysterious preference for tartan. Gentle, and bewildered by life was Fräulein Schwartz; she had never been able to make up her mind about anything since the days of her childhood, and yet she had had to face grave decisions. She was incomplete, part of a philippine, the major portion of which was missing.

Her father had been a most learnèd professor—that is, learnèd in all save the getting of money. They had lived in a pleasant suburb of Dresden not far from the bridge called "Der Blaue Wunder." As a child she had frequently stood on that bridge and gazed down at the Elbe, feeling rather afraid, gripping her father's protective hand, so impressed had she been by the depth of the water. After his death, when she was past thirty, she had dutifully wished to support her mother by teaching English, God save the mark! She had failed, which was not in the least surprising, for among those problems that had always bewildered her most might be counted the English language. But indeed she had tried a number of things for nine years, until she had lost her mother: fine needlework; knitting thick, gaudy stockings for the muscular legs of those who climbed mountains; even serving in a shop had Fräulein Schwartz tried, but not one of her ventures had been successful. Yet now here she was giving German lessons in London, and actually making a living.

Fräulein Schwartz was the friend of all the world, a fact which naturally made her feel lonely, since the world had no time for Fräulein Schwartz, nor had it expressed the least wish for her friendship. She loved children and after them animals; but children had never found her amusing. Stray dogs liked her, and sparrows would feed from her hand—but this only if the weather were frosty. Her true romance never having been born, she must cherish the memory of her parents, of her childhood, of her distant Fatherland; her large Bible resembled a photograph album. And let no one presume to despise Fräulein Schwartz if her links with the past were connected with eating. Why not? The bread that is broken in love, in guileless enjoyment and simplicity, may sometimes become as manna from Heaven. And although her mouth watered a little, it is true—she had suffered long years of boarding-house cooking—her eyes watered still more for the innocent days that were gone past all earthly hope of recalling.

Zwieback and a glass of fine, creamy milk . . . a spring morning in a tidy suburban garden; the witch-ball supported on stiff iron legs, a large luminous sphere reflecting the world, itself as immense as the world in proportions. Two earthenware dwarfs with curly grey beards; friendly, affable dwarfs clasping circular bellies: "Liebchen, do not make all those crumbs on the cloth; eat more carefully. What will the little men say? They are surely much grieved by untidy children!"

Apfelkuchen, always sweeter than sweet and tasting of the good, honest smell of ripe apples . . . the confectioner's shop in the Prager Strasse to which she had been taken on her sixth birthday. A smiling young salesman behind the counter who, when he had learned of the great occasion, had behaved as though she were really grown up and had actually called her: "Gnädiges Fräulein."

Schinkenbrot, crisp rolls stuffed with tender

pink ham . . . picnics to Bastei with her parents
in summer. The stout little steam-boat, so busy, so
willing. The songs they would sing steaming home
in the evening: "Lorelei," because they were on
the river, and sad old folk-songs because happy
people will not infrequently sing about sadness.

Pumpernickel, the delectable sticky black bread
. . . her mother cutting it into thin slices. Her
mother's spreading and matronly hips, so reassur-
ing beneath the check apron: "Nein, Liebchen,
you must wait for your Pumpernickel."

Wiener Schnitzel, fried slices of juicy veal; a dish
well beloved of her learnèd father. The dining-
room of their suburban home . . . a tiled stove of
such aggressive dimensions that it all but ousted
the dining-table. Her father, big, bearded and very
blue-eyed, a kind of paternal and ageing Siegmund,
bending over his plate of Wiener Schnitzel.

The hot spiced wine of All Hallowes E'en, and
the childish games that would follow after.
Flushed cheeks—that hot spiced wine was so
strong—and a great deal of mirth when she and
her friends must evoke ancient spells, each to get
her a husband. Her father and mother holding
hands, grown young again thanks to the hot
spiced wine. They had been middle-aged just as
she was now, and how strange that seemed—the

142

kind father and mother.

And those little brown loaves of marzipan that invariably made their appearance at Christmas. Ach, du liebe Zeit, Christmas! The old market-place as fragrant and green as a miniature forest. Rich and poor alike buying Christmas trees and driving away with them then and there in old country carts or fine equipages. Snow and sun-shine; the lake in the park frozen over, the band playing a waltz, the curvings and swayings of endless rosy-cheeked, bright-eyed skaters. Little ice sleighs, fashioned like gaudy birds. That fine pair of new skates with the curling fronts—what a lot they had cost. Ach, du liebe Zeit! she had surely possessed the most generous parents. Christmas day with its careful family presents; so much love had gone into each one with the making. Christmas night and the tree lighted up in the window just in case some poor creature outside should feel lonely: "Töchterchen, raise the blind before we light up—ja, so! Töchterchen, we should always remember the sad people who cannot have Christmas trees . . ."

Remember! Fräulein Schwartz could hardly forget since now she herself was one of those people. Sentimental? Perhaps. But then Fräulein Schwartz had always been incurably sentimental.

2

Whether it was Providence who sent her a present, or Chance, is a very difficult question; but the fact remains that returning from a walk one Christmas Eve, Fräulein Schwartz found a kitten on the doorstep of Raymond's Private Hotel. It mewed; it looked at her with anxious blue eyes; it had draggled grey fur and a very pink nose; it was young, it was starving, and it needed protection.

Fräulein Schwartz's defrauded maternal heart leaped up at this sight: "Armer Kerl!" she exclaimed. Then she gathered the kitten into her arms and proceeded to warm it under her jacket.

"You can't bring that thing in," Mrs. Raymond said firmly; "I won't have a kitten messing up all my carpets."

"Vhat you zay?" enquired Fräulein Schwartz. "But he starve, he is young and he also needs me."

"You can't bring him in," Mrs. Raymond repeated, "it's a rule of this hotel not to take people's pets."

"Dat is rubbish!" said Fräulein Schwartz, equally firm. And then: "I inzist dat I bring him in." And her pale Teuton eyes were so bright and

144

so fierce, and her thick Teuton voice was so pregnant with battle that Mrs. Raymond was completely nonplussed for a moment, and that moment gave her boarder the victory. "I go buy him a tray and some nice zoft zand; he be clean, you vill see," coaxed Fräulein Schwartz; for the beast's sake now bent on conciliation.

So the kitten was carried upstairs to her bedroom and was fed and caressed and generally tended. And its name, from that evening on, was Karl Heinrich, in memory of a very learnèd professor: "For," said Fräulein Schwartz, as she combed its thin fur, "der liebe Vater vould never object, and you haf his blue eyes—so clear and so childish. Jawohl, I vill certainly giff you his name." Then feeling a little doubtful she warned: "But remember, dat name is a ferry great honour!"

This had been between five and six months ago, and now Karl Heinrich was growing up daily. He had changed his milk teeth, and had visited the vet. for the purpose of sacrificing his manhood. He had learned that all carpets demanded respect and that Mrs. Raymond would see that they got it. He had learned that sparrows were hatched to be fed and not necessarily to be eaten; whereas mice, could one catch them, were considered fair game—though Fräulein Schwartz never praised him for mousing. He was learning that Alice, the parlour-maid, was one of those incomprehensible people who feel sick when a cat strolls into the room, and who consequently abhor the whole species. There was so much to learn with first this, then that, and yet life seemed wonderfully good to Karl Heinrich.

As for Fräulein Schwartz, it was really surprising what a difference his advent had brought about in her. She felt so much less lonely now at the thought that when she got home from work he would be waiting; that his food must be given, his coat brushed and combed, his ears looked to in case he be threatened with canker, his blue eyes watched for conjunctivitis, his temperature taken at least once a week, because being young he might get distemper—love, and a handbook on how to rear cats, had made her as crafty as any vet. Thus it must be conceded that Providence or Chance had been right in this choice of a Christmas present. For Fräulein Schwartz whose heart was so burdened with that large overload of maternal affection, Fräulein Schwartz the unwanted friend of all the world, was now wanted at last by a living creature. While Karl Heinrich, although, of course, as a cat who could trace his descent from a deity of Egypt, he could not quite sink to the level of a dog with lickings and wooffings and foolish

146

tail-waggings; although he must stalk in the opposite direction, head in air, tail erect, when his owner called him—this just as a matter of etiquette —Karl Heinrich had grown to adore that owner, and his purr when he rubbed his sleek length against her skirt would be vibrant and long with controlled emotion.

"Ach, du viel geliebtes Ding . . . ," she must frequently murmur, kneeling down to stroke his grey comeliness. "Ach, du mein Schatz," and other fond words she must speak to the cat in her guttural German.

And whether it was purely imagination—the imagination of a Fräulein Schwartz who was only too anxious to find compensations—or whether, as she sometimes assured Mr. Winter, Karl Heinrich did really struggle to respond, making queer and very uncatlike sounds while blinking his eyes as though from great effort; whether all this was true mattered not in the least, since it gave such deep pleasure and consolation.

3

Between Alan Winter and Fräulein Schwartz there existed a kind of companionable liking.

They met very seldom except at meals, but when they did meet they always felt friendly. He pitied her and she pitied him.

He would think: "It's hard lines to be growing old and to have no real home—only this putrid place. I wonder what will happen when she's really old; her sort never manage to save much money."

And she would be thinking how tired he looked, and how young he was to be so quiet and staid, and would long to teach him the student songs that she had been taught by her learnèd father, and would long to see him drink pints of beer, good iced beer —this in spite of his chronic dyspepsia. And though neither expressed sympathy for the other, since both of them were extremely shy people, yet they sometimes stopped if they passed on the stairs, stopped to talk for a little about Karl Heinrich. And Alan bought a ball on elastic which Karl Heinrich could make swing backwards and forwards, striking it deftly with soft, padded paws—a game that he found to be very amusing. And Fräulein Schwartz bought a bottle of tablets which the chemist assured her would cure indigestion, and she gave them to Alan who threw them away, but who, nevertheless, lied manfully when she asked him if he were not feeling better.

Thus the days drifted by. Fräulein Schwartz

taught German and Alan Winter slaved at his office; Mr. Pitt ran round and round Richmond Park, and Mr. Narayan Dutt went to lectures; and the Colonel was distant to the Misses Trevelyan, and the Misses Trevelyan were cold to the Colonel, and Mrs. Raymond played bridge with her guests every evening, but methodically underfed them, and no one believed that a war could come, despite ominous hints that appeared in the Press.

"The world is now governed by high finance, the financiers would never permit such a thing," said Mrs. Raymond complacently . . . a view that was shared by even the Colonel.

4

The night after England's declaration of war Alan Winter returned from the City dead-beat. His head ached and he had a dull pain in his chest. All day the office had been in confusion, all day he had struggled to grasp the fact that this war, which seemed like an evil dream, might become for him a reality.

"But I cannot go out there and kill," ran his thoughts. And then: "Is it that, or am I a coward? Am I really afraid of being killed?" A question to which he had found no answer.

Raymond's Private Hotel was blazing with lights. He could hear the sound of excited voices as he vainly tried to escape to his room: "Is that you, Mr. Winter?" called Mrs. Raymond. "We've been waiting up for you. Well, what's the news? Come and tell us what they say in the City."

Amazing the futilities that worried these people, he could scarcely credit his ears as he listened: what was likely to happen to trustee stocks, to consols and other gilt-edged investments? What was meant by national bankruptcy—did the City think it was likely to happen? And the income-tax; what did the City think?

Alan shrugged his thin shoulders, hating them all: "I can't tell you because I don't know," he snapped.

Colonel Armstrong eyed him malevolently: "This," said the Colonel, puffing out his chest, "this, in my opinion, is Armageddon!"

And then it began. They argued, they disputed, they grew bitter towards the Kaiser and each other. Quiet people, hurled violently out of their ruts, their nerves had been jarred and their tempers suffered. It was natural enough, the whole thing was so strange—so terrifyingly sudden and strange; for the moment they buzzed like angry

flies who were caught in the grip of some monstrous spider. Given time they would find their
dignity again, but just for the moment they lost
their tempers. Colonel Armstrong resented the
Misses Trevelyan's irritating allusions to the
senior service. The Misses Trevelyan retaliated by
asking impertinent, personal questions. Mr. Pitt
of the Y.M.C.A. called for vengeance upon every
head wearing a Prussian helmet. Mr. Narayan Dutt
smiled enigmatically and remarked that such
sentiments did not sound Christian; while Mrs.
Raymond, tired out and much worried, inveighed
hotly against the food profiteers, declaring that she
might have to put up her prices.

Some recent arrivals, a young couple from
Norfolk, brought a stock of the most disconcerting
rumours. The Germans had perfected Napoleon's
idea and built rafts—they might shortly be landing
at Dover; residents had been warned and were
leaving the town which would be defended by an
army of Russians. Food would soon become
scarce; they might have to eat rats as the starving
had done in the Siege of Paris—Mrs. Wilson knew
for a positive fact that the Government was going
to commandeer chickens. Queer people had been
met with all over the Broads, two such persons
were drifting about in a wherry; spies of course, all

England was riddled with spies and the police doing less than nothing about it. The Germans had bottled innumerable germs, anthrax and cholera germs among others, and these they would scatter in buses and tubes, spreading infection throughout the whole country. The navy was bristling with enemies, some of whom were flaunting their German names—Prince Louis of Battenberg, for instance; it was common knowledge that he would be shot, or at least arrested and put in the Tower—Mrs. Wilson hoped it would be in a dungeon. Spies were everywhere, not a corner was safe; why, the great wireless station quite near Llandudno had been run by a German man for years; he called himself Smith, but was really Schmidt. Mrs. Wilson's uncle lived down in those parts and had long had his eye on this dangerous fellow. But the real peril lay much less in the men than in the vast, secret army of women; female spies masquerading as ladies' maids, private secretaries, and even as teachers. They had wormed their way into important houses where, of course, they had overheard conversations. And not to be outdone, Colonel Armstrong, Mrs. Raymond, the Misses Trevelyan and Mr. Pitt, must produce even more startling contributions, so that to hear them was to feel little doubt regarding the ultimate fate of the Empire.

Then Mr. Pitt of the Y.M.C.A. stood forth as the champion of civilisation; and his strong duplex spectacles catching the light, seemed to glow with the flames of his righteous wrath as he spoke of the brutal invasion of Belgium; of the broken treaty, the iron heel, the will to destroy a defenceless nation; of the Kaiser puffed up with arrogance like the blasphemous Beast of Revelation. Merciless they had been, those invading hordes, yes, and well prepared for their devilish work:

"God pity the women and children," said he; "this sort of thing isn't civilised. They'll stop at nothing, you mark my words. I'd like to exterminate the whole brood, yes, I would; they don't deserve anything else. What they need is total extermination!"

He was kind and extremely placid by nature, and on the whole quite a passable Christian. He had never handled a rifle in his life or done bodily ill to a living creature. He had certainly run round and round Richmond Park in a harmless desire for physical fitness, but prize-fights had always made him feel sick—he had said many times that they were degrading. But to-night something potent had gone to his head, something that was in the very air he was breathing, so that he demanded an eye for an eye, forgetting the crucified God of his Gospels. And although he did pity the women and children and sincerely believe in his own good intentions, although, Heaven knew, there was reason enough to cry out against this thing that had happened, Mr. Pitt was not solely stirred by the wrongs and the agonies of an invaded Belgium. For side by side with his genuine pity and his quite justifiable indignation, lurked an instinct that was very unregenerate and old—mild Mr. Pitt of the Y.M.C.A. was seeing red, as a long time ago some hairy-armed cave-man had done before him.

Alan said abruptly: "I'm going upstairs."

His head was now aching beyond endurance. He was weary unto death of Mr. Pitt, of the Wilsons, of the Colonel, of them all, for that matter. He wanted to put the war out of his mind, if only for a few blessèd hours during sleep. Without saying good-night he turned and left them.

And away in a corner of the drawing-room, alone, stupefied, for the moment forgotten; half convinced that her country had committed a crime, and yet yearning painfully over that country; credulous one minute, incredulous the next, as she clung to the memory of her parents, of the Germany that she had once known—diligent, placid, child-loving and simple; a land of fairy tales,

Christmas trees, and artless toys fashioned for little children—away in a corner of the drawing-room sat Fräulein Schwartz, weeping large childish tears which dripped on to her tartan silk blouse unheeded.

5

England settled in to the grim stride of war. The Empire had swayed but had quickly recovered. Food rose sharply in price but nobody starved. A moratorium strengthened the banks which, despite Colonel Armstrong's fears, remained solvent; although after a time little, mean paper notes were to take the place of their weighty gold sovereigns.
. Fellow clerks at Alan's office enlisted and their posts were soon filled by adventurous women, all anxious to do their bit for their country, all anxious to learn, yet impatient of learning. But Alan, the victim of his treacherous nerves, of his body that had failed him ever since childhood, of his horror of blood and of violent deeds, above all of his vivid imagination, Alan held back and did not respond to the loud bugle call of Kitchener's army.

Mr. Pitt of the Y.M.C.A. was in khaki. He had

twice been refused on account of bad eyesight, but had managed to get himself taken at last, and this was immediately made the excuse for a very unworthy campaign of baiting. Alan was a handy and obvious butt, sitting all day on a stool in safety. The Misses Trevelyan cut him dead when they met; Colonel Armstrong—himself much too old to serve—made frequent and barbed patriotic allusions. Even Mrs. Raymond, try though she might to remember that Alan paid his bills promptly, that he seldom if ever complained of the food, the economy in fires or the tepid bath water, even Mrs. Raymond now viewed him askance, and if she addressed him at all did so coldly.

It was true that he was not the only blot, there was Fräulein Schwartz to whom nobody spoke except Alan, who felt very pitiful of her. There was also Mr. Narayan Dutt of Bengal—he had suddenly decided to leave the hotel, which the Misses Trevelyan thought highly suspicious. But then, as young Mrs. Wilson remarked with more force than refinement: "He's a yellow-belly!" Mr. Wilson was being drilled down in Cornwall where his wife was daily expecting to join him. It was not very pleasant, indeed, quite the reverse, but Alan would not let his thoughts dwell on these people; after all, he was fighting on the business front, and

England's motto was: "Business as usual!"

But if Alan's position was not very pleasant, Fräulein Schwartz's position was becoming desperate, for who in their senses would wish to learn German? Moreover, her very presence in the house was looked upon as a potential danger. Mrs. Raymond had already asked her to leave, but Fräulein Schwartz had protested with tears that, alas, she could find nowhere else to go to. For Fräulein Schwartz had but to open her mouth to arouse an immediate antagonism. One woman had banged the door in her face: "No, I 'aven't a room for the likes of you! Why don't yer go 'ome and stay with the Kaiser?" Yet cheap lodgings were an urgent necessity, since now she must live on her meagre savings.

Poor, ageing, inadequate Fräulein Schwartz, so anxious to be the friend of all the world yet so tactless in her methods of setting about it; for what must she suddenly try to do but perform little acts of unwelcome kindness, and this at a time when war-racked nerves would naturally lead to the worst interpretations. Mrs. Wilson was convinced that she was a spy, hence those crafty offers to help with the housework; she wanted, of course, to get the run of the place, hoping to unearth some information. Mrs. Wilson threatened to go to the police and was only dissuaded by Mrs. Raymond who declared that this might ruin her hotel, especially if it got into the papers. In the end Mrs. Wilson bought a miniature safe so that she could lock up her husband's letters.

Poor, ageing, inadequate Fräulein Schwartz; a more positive woman would have packed her trunks and tried to return to her native land. But the thought of that long and difficult journey, of passports, of frightening official delays punctuated by even more frightening questions, of a dwindling purse, and God knew what expense to be faced before she at last reached her country, had completely deprived her of her small stock of will, and so she had stayed on from week to week, innocent, blundering, bewildered and helpless.

Oh, but she was being crushed on the wheel, the fate of all those who are too tender-hearted. War, to her, seemed a great and most pitiful sin, even as it had to her learnèd father. It was said that her people did terrible things; it was also said that the English would starve them, two wrongs which could surely not make a right, and which left her more bewildered than ever. Each morning she prayed with great earnestness that God would bring peace to the warring nations; but at times God appeared to be very far off, so that she must seek a more present help in trouble. Getting up from her knees she would look at Karl Heinrich; then taking him on to her lap she would talk, for like most of her nation she dearly loved talking—indeed, she had suffered far more than they knew from the silence imposed by her fellow-boarders. And to all those deep problems which vexed her soul, Karl Heinrich would listen with infinite patience, though every recital would end much the same way: "Aber, vhat has gone wrong mit de vorld, Karl Heinrich?"

Karl Heinrich would find himself at a loss, since not even the wisdom of Ancient Egypt, as he very well knew, could have answered that question. And so he would start to sway his sleek tail, conscious of a disagreeable sensation in the region of the fur along his spine, for cats hate to be placed at a disadvantage. Then all that frustrated love of long years, all that urge to serve, all that urge to succour, all that will to protect the helpless of the earth, would Fräulein Schwartz pour out on her rescue. And since those whom we speak of as lesser creatures have their own quiet ways of divining our emotions, Karl Heinrich would cease from swaying his tail and would try to sit very still on her lap, so fearful was he of hurting her feelings.

Passing the door on her way downstairs, the parlour-maid, Alice, would pause to listen. And that low guttural voice would fill her with rage; with a senseless rage that made her feel giddy, so that now Karl Heinrich must suffer as well—they must suffer together, he and his mistress. Not that he was a German; he could prove that his father who frequented the backyards of Pimlico, had been born in a coal-cellar here in London. He could prove that his mother who lived five doors away had come into the world *via* a cupboard in Chelsea; all the same he must suffer from the girl's hostile eyes that made him feel intensely uneasy. Then again, she refused to bring up his food, declaring that the cook would no longer prepare it; and once she had given him a surreptitious kick, an outrage which he bore with philosophy, reflecting that Alice did not like cats—it seemed a just possible explanation.

Fräulein Schwartz must go out and buy milk in a can from the dairy and a loaf of stale bread from the baker; and on this meagre diet Karl Heinrich must live, since no scraps were available from the kitchen. But one day, although money was growing so scarce, Fräulein Schwartz bought Karl Heinrich a fine red collar; and she scratched his name on the plate with a pin—she had feared that

the shop might refuse to engrave it. Gentle she
was, and bewildered by life, yet this collar was in
the nature of a challenge.

"Can't abide the beast," Alice confided to
the cook, "and 'im belonging to that German
woman. Ought to kick the pair of 'em out of
the 'ouse. *And* 'is name! If she 'asn't gone
and scratched it on 'is collar. The impudence
of it, but then that's 'er! Any'ow the beast turns
me sick at me stomach."

Ah, yes, Alice was very bitter these days;
a little queer too and inclined to be spiteful,
for her wide muslin apron hid more than her
skirt. Much clasping in a thicket on Hampstead
Heath had resulted in what she hid under her
apron.

He had said: "Oh, come on! Ain't I goin'
to the front? Ain't I one of the 'eroes wot's
about to protect yer? 'Course I'll marry yer
when I gets 'ome on leave. But, Gawd, don't
go keepin' me 'angin' about . . ." And one
or two other things he had said; it had not been
at all a romantic seduction. So possibly Alice
was less to blame for her queerness than was
'Erb, and what he had called in his moments
of spiritual insight: "Nature."

6

Incredible of course that Fräulein Schwartz should have suddenly longed for her fellow-boarders, yet so it was, and the evening arrived when she could not endure coventry any longer; when tucking Karl Heinrich under her arm, she went down to the gloomy drawing-room and, much daring, broke into the conversation. Alan Winter, who had not as yet gone upstairs, was filled with a sense of impending disaster. What a moment to select, the poor tactless old fool! Hadn't she looked at the evening papers? They would think she had come to gloat over the news. And why bring the cat? His name was enough—a nice beast, but such an unfortunate name! Fräulein Schwartz had not seen any papers for days, indeed, she now frequently feared to see them.

She was trembling, already regretting her impulse, already regretting that she had brought Karl Heinrich. He would not sit still, he wanted to play and the chair had some very alluring buttons.

"Sieh' mal, dat is naughty—you must be a goot boy. Do not do it! Be quiet a little, Karl Heinrich."

She smiled awkwardly, glancing from face to face as a mother might do, half apologetic, half expecting a tolerant answering smile. But none came. Those animal-loving English could not find it in them to love Karl Heinrich—not just then, with the terrible lists of killed, of wounded and, more terrible still, of missing. Death and bereavement were everywhere now; no one in that room was nearly affected, yet bereavement had entered into the house. There had been a great noise of sobbing in the kitchen and the housemaid had had to serve the dinner that night. The girl had explained that some very sad news had reached Alice, hence those sounds of sobbing in the kitchen. And this German woman sat and played with her cat! It was true that she had not come down to dinner, that her room being at the top of the house she could not have heard what went on in the basement, nevertheless, she should have more shame; her presence was little short of an insult. No, they could not smile at the playful Karl Heinrich.

And he ought to have known better. He, so wise a cat, was being nearly as tactless as his mistress. What imp had got under his glossy grey fur and made him behave like a wilful kitten? Fräulein Schwartz's round forehead began to shine as she sweated with worry and mortification. And she talked, how she talked! It was almost as though her long enforced silence had left her bursting, so that now she must let loose a torrent of words. Alan thought as he listened that never before had he heard Fräulein Schwartz being quite so foolish or speaking in such abominable English.

"If only I could manage to stop her," he thought, glancing anxiously at their fellow-boarders.

They were doing their best. They were honestly trying to control their tongues and stifle their feelings; trying to answer her naturally, as though they were quite at their ease in her presence; trying in their unimaginative way to do the right thing, the dignified thing, on what to them was an odious occasion. But her thick Teuton voice jarred their every nerve, while her round Teuton face in their midst seemed an outrage when they thought of those wounded, missing, and dead. Quite suddenly they could not endure it and must start to castigate Fräulein Schwartz as if by so doing they struck at her country.

And now into the eyes of those quiet, dull people, crept a look that was unexpectedly cruel; the look of the hunter who corners his prey, watchful, alert with a sense of power—the power over life in the act of killing; while into Fräulein Schwartz's pale eyes came the puzzled, protesting

look of the hunted. Then Fräulein Schwartz
plunged, committing a blunder more grotesque
than any that had gone before it. In her genuine
will towards peace on earth, in her genuine conviction that all men are brothers, in her genuine
distress at the miseries of war, she must try to make
everyone there understand that she not only asked
for, but offered friendship. But they did not
understand; they mistook it for shame, since, alas,
in this world it is seldom wise to show the cross
hilt instead of the sword blade.

"Dere is someting I vant to zay," she was
stammering, "it is dis. Mein Vater vas against all
vars; he belonged to de Socialdemokraten, de
people's party, de party for peace. He thought var
vas a great und most pitiful zin . . . ach, ja, and I
feel as did my dear Vater. But ve here, ve hafe not
made de var, nicht wahr? It is not ve here who hafe
vished to make it. I am Cherman and derefore I
lofe my land; you are English and derefore you lofe
dis England; and I tink dat ve all hafe zo much
lofe in our hearts dat ve cannot help ourselves
lofing one another . . ." She paused, gasping a
little, but only for a moment, for now she was
carried away by her creed. She was holding up the
cross hilt of the sword and was strangely elated by
what she was doing, so that her voice when next

she spoke held in it the triumphant ring of the martyr: "Because of my country I hafe wept many nights. It is said dat our zoldiers hafe killed little children—I do not know. It is alzo said dat your English navy is going to starve us; you cannot starve only vomen und men, and derefore you alzo vill kill little children—I do not know. I know only dis, dat ve all should unite to stop zo much zuffering. Ach, listen! I feel dat de spirit of my Vater is in me here," and she struck her plump breast, "dat my Vater vants me to say dese tings; dat my Vater zays he implores you to listen. He zays dat in our dear countries to-night, dere are many goot people who feel as ve do, and dat if dey could dey vould stretch out dere hands and vould zay: 'Wir sind ja alle Brüder und Schwestern.'" Fräulein Schwartz stopped speaking; the light died from her eyes leaving them dull and curiously vacant.

Then a dreadful thing happened. Mrs. Wilson laughed shrilly; she laughed peal upon peal, for she could not help it, was indeed scarcely conscious of what she did—she was very near an hysterical breakdown. Fräulein Schwartz's face became ashen, and from one of those dimly lit chasms of the mind in which lurk the abhorrent and forbidden thoughts that engender great hatreds and great

disasters; in which lurk all the age-old cruelties that
have stood to the races for self-preservation; in
which lurk the hot angers of humbleness scorned,
and the blinding resentments that urge to vengeance; from one of those dimly lit chasms of the
mind there rushed up a mighty force fully armed,
and it gripped Fräulein Schwartz and possessed her
entirely, so that she who had been the friend of all
the world was now shaken by gusts of primitive
fury.

"Ach, accursèd English, you vhat laugh at de
dead; you who hafe not de heart vhat can feel
compassion! May be it is lies vhat you zay of our
men—yes—I tink it is you vhat kill vomen and
children. I tell you all vhat my Vater vould hafe
me, und you laugh, und you laugh at my dear dead
Vater! But may be you laugh less one of dese days
vhen our Uhlans ride through de streets of your
London. May be you laugh much less vhen our
ships blow up all of your cruel child-murdering
navy. Gott! I tink ve vas right to make zuch a
var; now I pray to Gott alvays dat He give us de
victory!" And gathering Karl Heinrich into her
arms she fled, while they sat stupefied and dumb-
founded.

But someone was watching as she lumbered
upstairs, clasping the cat to her heaving bosom.

Alice stood aside to allow her to pass—she had heard that impassioned, tempestuous outburst.

"So," she muttered, "so you 'opes as your bloody Germans is comin' to ride through the streets of London; the devils as 'ave made my baby a bastard and me nothing but an 'ore all the rest of me days. So that's what you 'opes, you foul German bitch. Well, I'll teach yer; so now you can go on 'opin'l" And Alice shook her trembling fist in the air, half demented by the thought of her coming child, the bitter fruit of a brutal deflowering.

7

The next afternoon being Saturday, Alan Winter returned from the office early. It struck him that the parlour-maid looked rather queer when she opened the door, but the thought soon passed. Alice, as he knew, had received bad news which would doubtless account for her strained expression.

Then stumbling downstairs came Fräulein Schwartz, her eyes red, her grey hair grotesquely dishevelled; and she clung to his sleeve, peering up at his face as though not very certain of her reception. But for all that she clung with tenacity.

"Gott sei Dank it is you and not one of de others . . ." she panted. And then: "Come quick up to Karl Heinrich!"

He stared at her, wondering if she had gone mad: "Karl Heinrich!" he repeated stupidly. He was tired, and his head was still heavy with figures.

She nodded: "Ach, Gott, he is terribly ill. If you vill not help me because I am Cherman, den help him, for he surely haf done notting wrong."

Alan thought: "And neither have you, you poor soul." Aloud he said: "I'll come up and see him."

They climbed the interminable stairs side by side, and as they did so she tried to explain how it was that Karl Heinrich had been brought so low; tried hard to keep calm and tell Alan the symptoms. It seemed that she had gone out to look for a room, and that on her return she had found him in convulsions.

"I do not know much, but I run to my book on de cat, und I tink it vere surely convulsions. . . . And vhen I look round he hafe been very sick . . . ach, but sick, sick, sick hafe he been in my absence. Und vhen de convulsions vas past come de pain, de 'orrible pain. . . . Ach, my poor Karl Heinrich! Und now dere hafe come de very great weakness. And I cannot understand; I myself buy his milch, und his bread I also buy from de baker, und no meat hafe he eaten for many days; und vhen I leave him to go hunt a room, he was vell as never before hafe I seen him. Herr Gott! Vhat has happened? Vhat can hafe befallen?"

Alan tried to soothe her as best he could, but he felt a queer sinking in the pit of his stomach and a sudden tightening across his chest: "Don't be frightened, it can't be serious," he soothed, "not if the cat was so fit when you left him . . ."

They had reached the top landing, he gasping for breath. The next moment she was pushing him into her bedroom. It was small and squalid, a despicable room, a disgrace to the house and to Mrs. Raymond. He had never been in it until that moment, and he saw it for the unhappy thing that it was: the sole refuge of a derelict human being. He supposed that there must be many such rooms in all cities, and many such derelict beings. Then his thoughts stopped abruptly—he had seen Karl Heinrich.

She had dragged the meagre pillow from her bed and had laid him upon it, just under the window. The beast seemed to have shrunk to half his size, and that was so queer—rather horrible even. And his glossy grey coat was now matted and dull. Some milk had stiffened the fur on his chest, spilt there when she had endeavoured to feed him. His whole body looked pitifully soiled but resigned, and Alan could feel its profound desolation. For seeing him thus, was to know that Karl Heinrich realised in some dim way that he was dying, and that he had not yet made friends with death—perhaps because he was still so young and had been very full of the joy of living.

Then Fräulein Schwartz sank on to her knees, not in prayer to God, but in love for His creature, and she slipped her arms under Karl Heinrich and rocked him as though she were rocking an ailing baby; and she murmured soft and consoling words, as though she herself were indeed a mother:

"Kleines Wörmchen, do not doubt und do not feel frightened. . . . Gott is kind, and all vill be vell, Karl Heinrich. He lofes you, for you are His little grey cat—tink of it dat vay, for Gott He made you. And I vill not leave you never, ach, nein, zo dat you shall not feel frightened und lonely. Can you hear me? Do you know I am mit you, Karl Heinrich? Ja, I tink dat you do, und dat it consoles you. Hafe great hope and fear notting at all, mein Schatz. . . . Zee, I shall alvays be very close." She appeared to have forgotten Alan Winter.

"Look here, I'm going for a vet," he said gruffly.

8

When he returned with the vet in half an hour, Fräulein Schwartz was sitting on the floor by the pillow. She was stroking Karl Heinrich methodically, and still talking—only now she was talking in German. For her mind had slipped back over many years to her mother and the days of her own young childhood, so that she was using little tricks of speech, half playful, half grave, and wholly consoling; so that she was telling of gnomes, but kind gnomes, and of other such folk who were all very kind; trying to lure Karl Heinrich away from the realms of pain into those of enchantment.

"Is she a German then?" whispered the vet.

Alan nodded: "She is, but the poor beast isn't."

The man flushed: "I'm a healer, not an Empire!" he said sharply.

Turning, he went to Fräulein Schwartz: "This gentleman has brought me to look at your cat. Do you mind if I make an examination? He's told me the symptoms. . . . I'm afraid they're pretty grave."

Fräulein Schwartz got clumsily on to her feet
and motioned to the vet to take her place. She
gave him a searching look but said nothing. With
gentle deftness he set about his task; lifting the
eyelids, opening the mouth, pressing his ear to the
beast's shrunken side, and listening again and
again for the heartbeats. But Karl Heinrich was
already a long way away; he had gone to the
country that needs no frontiers, and where wars
and the rumours of wars are forgotten.

The man shook his head: "I'm too late," he told
them, "but in any case I don't think I could have
saved him. In my opinion this cat's been poisoned."

"Poisoned? Oh, no, that's impossible! Who on
earth would have done such a thing?" exclaimed
Alan.

But Fräulein Schwartz spoke in an odd, hushed
voice: "If dat is de truth, den for me has he
suffered, and for my nation, und for all de nations
vhat zo cruelly go out to hurt vone another. Karl
Heinrich vas only a little grey cat vhat I rescue
vhen he vas cold und starving; but now Karl
Heinrich is very much more, he is zomething
enormous und terrible: a reproach before Gott who
vill not forget de zufferings of poor dumb beasts
und of children. I hafe maybe lost him for a little
vhile, ja. I hafe lent him to Gott, but only for a

little; because Gott, who hates var, vill give him me back. He vill say: 'Karl Heinrich hafe told Me about it; all de pain und de fear und de doubts vhat he felt before you come home in de end und find him, zo dat now he shall go again vhere he vould be, und dat is mit you—I gife back your Karl Heinrich.' "

The vet glanced at Alan uneasily: "I'd like to make an autopsy," he murmured.

But Alan shook his head: "Don't suggest it— no good—she's half crazy with grief, it would only distress her."

"But she can't keep him here. I could take the body . . ."

Fräulein Schwartz swung round: "Vhat is dat you are zaying? Aber nein; aber nein; I vill bury him myzelf."

"Well—I'm sorry I couldn't save him, Fräulein." The vet looked at his watch; there was nothing he could do, and moreover he had another appointment.

"If you'll come downstairs, I'll attend to your fee," muttered Alan, and he almost ran from the room, conscious only of a wild desire to escape from the blemished beast and the grief-stricken woman.

Alone with her dead, Fräulein Schwartz spoke to

God, and she told Him quite quietly about this
great sorrow, and about the troubles that had gone
before—her loneliness, her fears, her inadequacy,
and the feeling that life had denied her fulfilment.
She told Him of the wish she had always cherished
to befriend the whole world, to be one great heart
into which the whole world could creep for protection, and of how she had found that nobody
came, that nobody wanted her heart but Karl
Heinrich, who had thus in some strange way
become the whole world, which was surely God's
compassionate dispensation. Then she asked His
forgiveness for all her transgressions; for her anger
upon the previous evening and for all those
terrible things she had said—none of which she had
really meant, she assured Him. And for what she
would now do she asked it also if, indeed, according
to His wisdom it were sinful, which she could not
believe since none other than He had sent her this
very great love for Karl Heinrich.

"And I promise dat I vould not leave him, ach,
nein, because he is only zo helpless a ding vhat I
care for zince he vas a tiny kitten. Und he might
feel strange, even mit You, mein Vater im Himmel,
though I tell him of all Your kindness . . ."

For some reason she was praying in English, in
the thick Teuton English that made people angry,

that indeed, had nearly cost her her home—but perhaps God did not notice her accent. In any case she drew much comfort from her prayer and much courage; both excellent reasons for praying.

Presently, she was setting her bedroom in order, so that when they went in they should find it tidy; and this done she got money out of her trunk and left it on the table for Mrs. Raymond.

"Zo! Und now I owe nobody notting," she murmured, "I am glad, for had it been othervise, they vould all hafe zaid dat I paid not my rent because I vas vhat dey call: 'A damn Cherman.'" And she actually smiled a little to herself, not unkindly, but rather with a vague toleration.

Finally, she pinned on her shabby black hat, then she slipped her arms into an old tweed ulster—it was ample, almost too big she remembered, and thus it could easily shelter them both. Lifting the stiffening body of the cat, she buttoned it gently under the ulster.

Poor, ageing, inadequate Fräulein Schwartz; even at this stupendous moment when for once in her life she had made up her mind, when for once she was filled with a great resolve, even now she must walk lop-sided through the streets, looking as though some abominable growth had laid its distorting hand upon her; indeed, more than one person turned to stare at the odd little woman who walked so quickly. Quickly, yes, for she had a long way to go before she would come to that quiet place where the trees bent forward over the river; where the river was dark and brooding with peace. By the time she had reached it she would be very tired and glad of her sleep, for the night would have fallen. Karl Heinrich was already fast asleep —she could feel him lying against her bosom.

THE REST CURE—1932

Mr. Duffell sat at his mahogany desk. He was painfully striving to focus his attention on the papers that he had brought home from the office: invoices, engineers' reports, the auditors' report, urgent letters from the bank. And as he sat there in his study alone, the ormolu clock on the mantelpiece struck midnight.

Mr. Duffell was conscious of a weariness so vast that it seemed to permeate his whole being, so that it was anguish to know himself alive, and yet since he was alive work he must, and that with alacrity and precision. Mr. Duffell goaded his flagging mind, and as he did this there came an odd pain that played over his head like a flash of forked-lightning —a bright, zigzag, disconcerting kind of pain that passed quickly; he had felt it once or twice before and had thought it some form of acute neuralgia. As a rule his mind would respond to the goad, but to-night it was being recalcitrant and stubborn, shying away from those papers on the desk and galloping off in another direction. He swore softly, filled and lighted his pipe, grasped a pen and tried to check a report, but the figures meant nothing to him at all, the results he produced were obviously nonsense.

He began to see pictures, mental pictures, very much as though he were drowning. He saw himself lashing a whipping-top, he saw himself feeding a spaniel puppy, he saw himself kneeling in the chapel of his school, he saw himself scrambling on to a roof during a memorable rag at Oxford. And, later he saw himself grimy and hot in the vast workshops of Duffell & Son, learning to become a master of men by first becoming the least among them.

Then the pictures changed, growing more panoramic—those years that had followed his father's death, how calm they had been; calm, successful years during which he had decided never to marry, had decided that a wife would be in the way of a man already wedded to business. And the war . . . it had brought fine profits to the firm, profits honestly earned, for Duffell & Son produced only of the best—their steel was world-famous. Had it not been said that Duffell & Son had helped to link up the British Empire? The war —their magnificent Roll of Honour: "The following died for King and Country." How proud he had felt as he read those names; he himself had laid an immense laurel-wreath at the foot of the handsome and glorious tablet; that had been on the second Armistice day—a laurel wreath bearing the Allied colours.

And then what? The lame, the halt and the blind; abominable treaties; a shrinkage of commerce at first gradual but gaining bewildering momentum with every fresh greedy and witless blunder. A world at war then a world at peace, more cankered by the so-called peace than by war—a world full of angers, suspicions and confusions, a world of black hating and blacker self-seeking, a world that had savagely turned upon itself as it writhed in the flames of its own perdition. And he, Charles Duffell, shocked and confounded by the crashing of almost every landmark that had hitherto served as a guide in business. He, Charles Duffell, honest, thrifty, astute—a fair man but no fool when it came to a deal—he floundering about far out of his depth as he struggled to swim against the current, to restore to the firm its dwindling reserves while not reducing the pay of his workmen.

Then the visit to business connections in New York, how clearly he remembered every detail of that visit: the well-nigh fantastic prosperity, prices challenging heaven like the soaring skyscrapers; the optimism of the man in the street, his childlike

faith in the present and future; his belief that the
rest of the world could go hang and America still
continue to prosper; his conviction that clever old
Uncle Sam had turned himself into a modern
Aladdin. And that delirious orgy of speculation—
every Tom, Dick and Harry having a fling, even
down to the impudent hotel bellhop. The germs of
the illness so thick in the air that only to breathe was
to catch the infection—he had caught it at once,
yes, and caught it badly. Looking back it appeared
incredible that a staid and experienced man of
affairs should have hoped thus to add vast sums to
his fortune, yet so it had been, he had hoped for
just that, he had hoped to pump golden blood into
Duffells.

When the crash came in the autumn of 1929, he
had been on board ship returning to England. He
could see himself as he paced the long decks of that
huge and insolent luxury liner. And those others
who had paced her decks he could see—they had
none of them lacked for news, thanks to progress!
The atrocious strain of those days in mid-ocean,
the faces of men who had lost their all, who had
left their country as millionaires and who must
return to their country as paupers; their incredulous
amazement at this brutal deception, the stony
despair that had followed after—these things were

184

burnt into Mr. Duffell's brain, so that he shrank from the memory of them, and yet as he sat at his mahogany desk must live over again that terrible autumn. And the years that followed he must also live over, three years of incessant anxiety; of hope lifting a timid and battered head as the prophets whose wish was father to the thought had babbled of the coming business revival—of the business revival that never came. And somehow those moments of perverse optimism had been far more unmanning and far more cruel than the months of well-nigh unrelieved gloom, at least so it appeared to Mr. Duffell, and he cursed the false prophets, wishing them ill with all that was left of vitality in him.

But insomnia. Never until now had he known how hallowed and precious a gift was sleep, how hellish the nights could be without it. Sleep was surely worth all the gold in the banks, yet all the gold in the banks could not buy it. A man might drug himself with a whore, only to start wide awake in revulsion; a man might try to buy sleep at his chemist, only to feel like death the next morning. Ah, no, not by such means could a man hope to woo the sleep that revitalised mind and body. And doctors—what fools when they weren't knaves: "You need rest, my dear sir, and of course no worry. My advice is to go for a long sea voyage, leaving your business to take care of itself. Cut loose from it all for at least six months." Cut loose from it all for at least six months, when every moment you were urgently needed, when every moment some new trouble cropped up! And how in hell's name could a man find rest when wherever he went these days there was noise: the roaring of aeroplanes over his head, the incessant hooting and throbbing of cars, the blaring of those infernal loud-speakers? And yet it was an agony to feel so tired that one actually dreaded having to shave, actually dreaded the effort of dressing. . . . If only one need not see, need not hear, need not be conscious of movement and sound; if only a man could lie absolutely still in a universe of invulnerable stillness. . . .

The clock struck four, and Mr. Duffell winced. He stared at the papers strewn about on his desk: "I must go into these accounts," he muttered, prodding his mind yet again with the goad and prodding it now quite ruthlessly. "I must and will go into these accounts, I must and will save the firm. I must . . ."

His body went suddenly cold then hot, he sweated and while he did so he shivered. That odd zigzag pain played over his head with such violence that he screamed, clutching blindly at air; the next moment it was gone and his mind felt as clear as a crystal lake on a summer morning. Never before had he known such a feeling, such placidity, such a conviction of power, such a Godlike and omnipotent sense of detachment.

A blowfly woke up and began to buzz. "You see, it's like this," said Mr. Duffell, addressing himself to the drowsy insect, "it mustn't go on because it needn't. If it had to go on then doubtless it would, or rather I'd say that it might go on, but now, as it needn't, I say it mustn't. Anyhow, the whole thing is entirely absurd." He paused to wave the fly from his face. "You're much too fly-conscious," he told it gravely, "you're attracted to my particular nose which means that you think of me as a person, and of yourself as an entity having characteristic likes and dislikes—this, of course, is a very common mistake which, considering its logical sequence, is dangerous. What is Charles Duffell? The purest illusion. That's the reason why none of this need go on, why Charles Duffell himself need not go on . . . so easy, as he never really existed! IT was born and tradition labelled IT: 'Man.' IT might have been labelled anything else. IT might have been labelled: 'Tree,' for instance. 'And he looked up, and said, I see men as trees, walking.'

Undoubtedly, very significant words. . . . or IT
might have been given no label at all, in which case
IT could have controlled ITS own fate. Labels
should never be tacked on to Life, they are in the
nature of a challenge to God—God assures me that
he objects to labels.

"An IT with a label is naturally foredoomed, and
supposing the IT has been labelled human then so
much the worse—IT gets family ties bringing with
them another damnable label. Duffell, I became,
through my family ties—you see my so-called
parents were Duffells. A name is a frightful thing
to possess, from the first it imposes an intolerable
bondage, the bondage of traditions attached to
that name. I inherited the Duffell traditions. I
endured with patience because I believed that I was
a person called Charles Edward Duffell who was
head of a firm known as Duffell & Son, a firm of
almost unique importance. Illusion again—just
the purest illusion. What is personality after all
but a monstrous and vindictive mass-conception?
And what, for that matter, is Duffell & Son but the
monstrous conception of a certain George Duffell
who was labelled in 1829, and who passed his
chains on to his unhappy descendants? And yet
those chains are quite simple to break," Mr.
Duffell made a quick movement with his hands,

"like this—a slight twist and no more chains!

"As I have now ceased to be Charles Duffell, I have ceased to be bound by his obligations, I have ceased to be tired with his tiredness, or tormented out of my sleep by his worries. His affairs are no longer my concern. . . . Of course they are no concern of anything's really, because—as is practically the whole mad scheme—his affairs are just one of those mass conceptions like poverty and wealth, the value of gold, international exchanges and other such bubbles. One thing only is indisputably real and that's Life. We are forced to believe in Life, and moreover, that it is regrettably eternal."

Mr. Duffell switched out the lamp on his desk: "Dear me," he remarked, "the sun is up." Then grasping a ledger he crushed the blowfly; after which he shaved and had a hot bath—he felt unexpectedly hungry for breakfast.

*　　　*　　　*　　　*　　　*

Mr. Duffell was on his way down to Cornwall. Had you been sharing his first-class compartment you would have seen a middle-aged man of medium height and inclining to stoutness, a man with slightly protruding brown eyes, a firm mouth and a broad, well-proportioned brow. From his staid and unobtrusive grey suit, you might well have deduced that he was in business.

Mr. Duffell was reading the *Financial Times*, and apparently finding it very amusing, for he smiled continually as he read.

"Take your seats for luncheon!" called the dining-car conductor.

Mr. Duffell glanced up: "Why should I?" he questioned.

"Beg pardon, did you speak, sir?" The conductor paused.

"Tell me, why should we eat?" enquired Mr. Duffell.

The man looked startled: "I suppose, sir, to live . . ."

"Tell me, why should we live?" Mr. Duffell sighed.

"That I really can't say, sir. Excuse me, sir. . . . Take your seats, if you please, take your seats for luncheon!"

"He's as mad as a hatter," mused Mr. Duffell.

Presently, he folded the *Financial Times* and stared at his kit-bag with pride and pleasure. The bag was new as were also his clothes, neither bore any marks of identification. He was thinking: "I'm brand-new inside and out." Then he frowned, "but I mustn't go on saying I—the I is the cause of all the trouble."

Mr. Duffell had taken a ticket to Penzance, but when the train stopped at a wayside station he clutched his bag and jumped nimbly out: "Is there an inn round these parts?" he demanded. "Or failing that is there a good cattle-pen? Or failing that is there a beach umbrella?"

The porter objected to this type of wit: "The Commercial Hotel's down the street," he said glumly.

Mr. Duffell departed with a smile and a nod. He took short, quick steps and his walk was springy. He looked neither to right nor left as he walked, yet for all this he found the Commercial Hotel where he registered himself as: Tom Smith of Melbourne, engaged a bedroom, deposited his bag, and enquired at what hour the hotel served dinner. Then he went for a stroll beyond the town in order that he might plan the campaign that he meant to wage against Charles Edward Duffell.

He thought: "It's no good killing the fraud for death doesn't exist; besides, there's nothing to kill as Charles Edward Duffell has no real life. . . . I think, no, IT thinks that it must be his legs—two legs are so aggressively human, and that label immediately conjures up the I, and in ITS case the I suggests what IT was called—the I reminds IT of what IT was called . . ." Mr. Duffell's mind gave a jerk and he laughed: "Ho, ho! my fine fellow, IT'S got you!" he laughed, "IT knows that what you describe as: 'human,' is merely another of your ludicrous distinctions, therefore what is the only sane conclusion? That nothing is either human or sub-human . . . that nothing is really anything at all, and this being so, IT can be what IT likes!" Mr. Duffell felt an immense satisfaction.

He strolled on, and presently he came to a field in which stood a couple of handsome young horses; one of them suddenly lay down and rolled, kicking its four neat hooves in the air. Mr. Duffell stood watching these proceedings for a moment, then he gravely removed his coat and waistcoat, placed them under the hedge, climbed the stile into the field, walked towards the horses on hands and toes, and finally started rolling himself. The horses galloped away in terror.

Mr. Duffell sat on his heels and considered. It was clear that the horses had labelled him: "Man"; he remembered that the blowfly had done this also. Not nearly so easy as he had supposed, to divest the IT of Charles Edward Duffell, and could this be done, as of course it could, how prevent an equally tiresome illusion, the illusion of the horses that the IT was a horse and as such something rather less than a man? Did animals perceive that they too

wore labels? How far did the animal consciousness
go? Mr. Duffell thought he would like to find out.
Of course animals had nerves and nerves played
odd tricks—nerves were often the most almighty
deceivers. It was clear that these creatures had
been deceived . . . how appalling this universal
deception! Now what was the strongest link
between ITS in their physical state—between
groups of ITS? Surely Life. And what was it that
kept Life alive? Surely food—without food no
bodily existence. Mr. Duffell nodded; how simple
it all was—questions and immediately the right
answers! Not the food of the gods, but the food of
the horse. . . . "By their bellies shall they find
themselves united." He dropped down again on
his hands and toes, and bending his face to the sod
he grazed, but something seemed wrong with the
shape of his jaw. And his teeth were completely
inadequate, when he tore up some grass he could
not chew it, and when he swallowed a blade un-
chewed it stuck in his throat and he nearly choked.
Coughing and gasping he got to his feet.

"Damn!" Mr. Duffell gasped, "damnation!"
Then he stooped and struck the grass violently:
"You look out, or I'll set you on fire!" he threat-
ened.

An hour later he was sitting in the hotel

coffee-room, a middle-aged gentleman eating his dinner.

*   *   *   *   *

That night Mr. Duffell could not sleep; insomnia held him once more in its clutches, and when he endeavoured to stifle thought his brain became ferociously active. Had there ever been known so active a brain, or one possessing such lucid vision? For now Mr. Duffell's mind was alight with what seemed to him a most terrifying problem, the problem of everlasting life. He had thought of it calmly enough by day, but alone in the darkness he groaned aloud:

"I'm too tired to live for ever . . . too tired. I want to go out like my candle went out. Please, please, I want to go out . . ." he prayed, "let me go out. I'm so dreadfully tired."

Life, always Life; always more and more Life. Billions of eels the size of pins, and they never came to maturity, they died while they were the size of pins. . . . And yet because God was indestructible Himself, He could only create the indestructible; His power fell short of obliteration. How appalling to be an indestructible God unable to stop the wheel of torture. Rolling . . . a wheel . . . no, not a wheel; surely it was the earth that rolled? Or

did it spin—did it spin like a top? The earth spun
round the sun like a top. Then whatever one did
one would never find stillness. . . . How could
one find stillness when the earth was a top? No
wonder so many people went mad—no wonder,
when they heard that terrific top humming.
Horror . . . he heard it! Hum, boom, hum . . .
it was like a vicious and fabulous bee, the sound of
it ached in his throbbing ears. He covered his ears
with his hands—still there. He buried his head
beneath the bedclothes—still there, still there! He,
too, would go mad! And movement . . . that was
why the whole house creaked; it was creaking in
rhythm with the spinning of the earth. . . :
Everything moved even when it seemed still . . .
stillness was the greatest of all the illusions. No
wonder he felt so painfully tired; even when he
slept he was never at rest because the earth was
never at rest, and like Life this devilish spinning
was eternal. What did it matter about those labels?
What did anything matter except this stark truth:
the earth spun round the sun like a top, and as it
spun it hummed like a top, and he could perceive
both the sound and the movement.

He sat up and began to thump his temples; then
he suddenly let his hands fall on the sheet and his
face became unbelievably cunning: "As I'm the

last person left who's sane, it's natural that I should be able to think," he said loudly, "should be able to find a way out. Silence, while I think. . . . Don't make so much noise!"

One thing was quite clear, the organism was solely responsible for all suffering, and the higher the organism the more nerves wherewith to apprehend and perceive, therefore better go down in the scale of creation. The lower one got the less one perceived, the farther one was from the source of Life—either transitory Life or Life everlasting. And the smaller the influx of Life the greater the rest. He had noticed that trees looked restful, perhaps because being rooted in the soil they were not much disturbed by perpetual movement—it must feel very safe to be rooted in the soil, if one's trunk were so anchored one might not get giddy.

He left his bed and tiptoed round the room. The dawn came palely in at the window. He intended to put his theory into practice—already that humming had grown much fainter and the house had stopped creaking. He slipped on some clothes, went downstairs and opened the front door with precaution.

Once out in the street he walked towards the field to which he had gone on the previous evening.

The little town was wonderfully still; it was smelling of dew on its red-brick pavements, and presently the lanes were smelling of earth and of things whose lives were rooted in the earth. Mr. Duffell sniffed the smell with contentment.

The horses were lying down when he reached them; Mr. Duffell was careful not to cause a disturbance: "Poor creatures," he thought, "let them sleep while they can, the IT that is me is kinder than God. . . . IT would never have created the world at all . . ." He paused to gaze sadly at the resting beasts, then passed over the field to the farther hedge where he halted.

"I am now a tree," said Mr. Duffell.

The sun came out brightly and dazzled his eyes— it made his eyes blink, but still he stood there. His body grew stiff from the strain of the pose he had forced it to take, but still he stood there. He had stretched his arms high above his head, and their flabby, inadequate muscles were aching; and one of his feet had gone to sleep—he was painfully conscious of pins and needles.

"Perhaps my foot's rooted at last," he thought, "perhaps what I feel is the coming of roots." With great caution he eased the foot from the ground but nothing detained it—his foot had not rooted. Then Mr. Duffell looked up at his fingers: "Where are your lovely green buds?" he asked them. "I think it's high time you began to bud." But his fingers remained unresponsive and naked. "Patience . . ." he sighed, "IT must have more patience . . . look at ITS brother tree over there, so fine a trunk didn't grow in a hurry."

At that moment the tree was stirred by a wind and while he watched it the wind grew stronger. The branches began to sway restlessly, and some leaves came drifting towards Mr. Duffell. Then Mr. Duffell heard the tree speaking, and this he did without any surprise.

"Do you think that we trees find rest?" said the tree. "You fool of an IT, do you think we find rest? Have you forgotten the winter storms? Trees are doomed to perpetual movement and noise. Then again, because we have sensitive roots we can feel the earth spinning even more than you can; and because every leaf that we bear has ears—little, but very acute green ears—we have hundreds and hundreds of little green ears with which to perceive that eternal humming."

Mr. Duffell's arms dropped limply to his sides: "Still a great deal too near the Life-force . . ." he muttered.

Leaving the field he walked on slowly, scarcely conscious of where the lane was leading until he came out on a stretch of moor—there were round, smooth stones on the moor, and heather. Mr. Duffell was drowning in a fathomless depression; it was like being thrust head downwards in a well that was full of turgid and icy water. He wanted to weep but no tears would come. Rubbing his eyes he tried to bring tears, but only succeeded in bruising his eyelids. His feet felt like lead, and his brain seemed clogged as though by slimy and foul-smelling mud. He was conscious of very great physical weakness. Sitting on a boulder he endeavoured to think. Then it was that he heard something inside his head—the sharp, staccato striking of a clock. It struck four times.

"Oh, my God!" cried Mr. Duffell, "oh, Christ Jesus . . . what am I doing in this place?" At that moment Mr. Duffell knew the meaning of hell, then the darkness descended again like a curtain.

When next he spoke he did so to a stone that his fingers were tapping automatically: "I believe you're the nearest thing to extinction, the farthest away from the Life-force," he told it, "in you there surely can't be much Life—at all events not enough Life to count, and that being so you don't see and don't hear. You're nerveless and quite unconscious of movement. As you'll still be a stone in Eternity, you've got less to dread through being eternal. You're naked and hard and insensitive. I hadn't thought of becoming a stone . . ."

* * * * *

"But where is the man?" enquired the policeman.

"Up there on the moor," replied the labourer, "he's all humped together, it's awful queer, and he's kind of curled round—never saw such a thing—and when I spoke to him he didn't answer."

"Kicked the bucket, probably," said the policeman.

"Not he! He's alive, you may take my word. But you'd better come quick—the blighter's stark naked!"

* * * * *

"I'm a stone," explained Mr. Duffell politely, feeling that he owed an explanation to the burly stranger with the affable smile. "I'm one of those large, smooth, circular stones that to all intents and purposes are dead . . . not completely dead for there is no death, but so nearly dead that they might be entirely."

The attendant eyed the new patient with interest, then because geology had long been his hobby:

"Well, now, I don't know about stones being dead. I've cracked open a stone and found a crystal; if that don't show life, then I'll eat my hat! It must take a bit of doing to form those crystals. To my way of thinking a stone's full of life; why, I've heard that some stones bring good or bad luck, just as if they had their likes and dislikes—almost, you might say, as though they could feel . . ."

Mr. Duffell shrieked. "Don't say it!" he shrieked, and he went on shrieking more and more loudly, and his hands shot out to seize the man's throat, but the man was too quick for those clawing hands. Another attendant rushed up, and together they overpowered and bound Mr. Duffell.

"Look at that now!" said the aggrieved attendant. "Whoever would have thought that he'd have turned nasty."

UPON THE MOUNTAINS

I HAD not seen Giulio Santaspina for some years; not, in fact, since I left the British Embassy at Rome, but when we met quite by chance at the Berkeley, we did so as old friends who were glad to see each other, and I asked him to share my flat on Hay Hill for the few days that he remained in England. It was during that visit that Santaspina told me the story of the della Valdas—an unusual story, I must admit, though perhaps I found it less strange than he did.

Santaspina is a Neapolitan by birth, which probably accounts for the deep sense of drama that he managed to impart to his narrative; a sense of drama that struggled at times with the scepticism of the modern Italian. Once or twice as the story approached its climax his voice sounded awed; he is very superstitious in spite of his vaunted modernity and his obvious wish to appear a sceptic.

I may not succeed in making the thing live as Santaspina did when he told it in his own expressive and lovely language; written down and in English it may well seem less real, but this I must risk because of the urge that has suddenly come upon me to write it.

We were sitting alone in my library one evening discussing Roman society as it was in the old days before the war, and I naturally spoke of the della Valdas, who had both been so popular and so much sought after.

"What's become of Valentino and Matteo della Valda?" I asked.

Santaspina was silent a moment. And then: "Dead . . . both dead," he replied sombrely, "but not killed in the war, either of them," he added.

I became so familiar with death at the Front that the thought of it has long ceased to impress me, yet when it was mentioned in this connection—in connection with these two young Roman brothers —I stared at Santaspina incredulously, feeling a curious sense of outrage. That death should have smitten down Valentino and his brother Matteo who was one year his junior, unless in battle, struck me as grotesque. They had always appeared so intensely vital: Valentino with his clear olive skin, his dark eyes that would constantly shine with enthusiasm, his slim wiry body, his sensitive mouth, his expressive hands and his passion for music; Matteo, fair-skinned, fair-haired and blue-eyed; an athlete, an intrepid mountaineer, a fine horseman, and carrying off his great height with the perfect poise of strong, supple muscles.

Matteo had belonged to a cavalry regiment, as indeed Valentino should also have done had he wished to uphold the family tradition. But Valentino had spurned the idea, perhaps rightly, for his talent was entirely creative. His ambition was to write an opera one day upon somewhat original lines, I believe—an opera that was to become world-famous.

When I heard that these young men were now dead, there arose in my mind a picture of them both as they had been at the time when I had first known them. I could see Valentino sitting at the piano and playing to us on a warm spring evening, I could see his sleek head thrown a little back, his dark eyes half-veiled by their finely modelled lids; and his hands, those expressive, long-fingered hands, striking out such strangely arresting chords . . . I could see Matteo, big, florid, protective, bending over his brother to turn the pages; turning them too soon or not soon enough, because he knew more about horses than music, but always insisting on this labour of love because it would keep him near Valentino. I could see the expression with which Valentino would glance up—a fond yet quizzical expression. "Like this

. . . . and this . . . and this!" he would say, and
Matteo would nod and try to look wise, at which
Valentino would burst out laughing.

Santaspina interrupted my thoughts. "I wonder
you did not hear about it all. Rome talked of
nothing else for months. I remember though that
you had left Rome for Teheran when it happened."

And then he told me.

*   *   *   *   *

"It happened in connection with a passion for
a woman and a passion for great heights; they do
not go well together, they did not in this case,
and both had their share in the deaths of Tino
and Matteo della Valda.

"You remember the devotion that there was
between those brothers, how each would always
defend the other, and how protective Matteo would
be though he was the younger. We used to tease
him. 'Nonna,' we called him, and he would just
grin and explain that the Blessèd Virgin was busy,
but that someone must keep an eye on Tino, who
was slightly erratic, being a genius. And you
probably knew that he was erratic, but what you
may very well not have known was that Tino's
artistic mode of life was intensely obnoxious to
his mother. The della Valdas were Black Catholics,

they had sacrificed much for the sake of the Church, and the old Marchesa had grown narrow and bitter. She mistrusted all artists and nearly all art as pandering to the world, the flesh and the devil. A kind of Savonarola she was, as stern and relentless to herself as to others. Imagine, therefore, her anger and chagrin when Tino insisted on studying music; when, moreover, he left the maternal home and took that apartment down by the Tiber. I, who had been her friend for many years, could judge of the severity of the blow—you see Valentino was the elder, the heir, and by rights he should have gone into the army. She was very strong-willed, but then so were her sons, and as usual Matteo sided with Tino.

"The Marchesa would sometimes talk openly to me—an indulgence which she seldom permitted herself—and I learned that she was irritated and puzzled by her sons because of their mutual devotion. 'They are two against one, it is disrespectful; they appear to forget that I am their mother. I have heard that some twins will behave in this way, but then they are not twins, a year lies between them.'

"And of course she was right, their devotion was amazing; I have never seen anything the least like it. If you can imagine a soul split in twain by separate bodies and resenting this rift in its unity, then you may get some idea of the thing as I saw it who had known the brothers all their lives, who had watched them grow from childhood to manhood. And it kept them pure; you will possibly doubt this, having lived for many years among Latins, nevertheless I am speaking the truth. They seemed armed against the assaults of the flesh, so that neither of them fell a victim to a woman—not until that summer of 1909, just after you had started for Teheran.

"That summer the Marchesa went to Bellaggio, where she opened up the family villa; and with her, as it happened, went both her sons. I went also, making one of a large house party. We were all very happy; the weather was perfect and the old Marchesa seemed far more human than I had seen her for a very long time. She appeared to be trying to understand Tino. Once she actually asked him to play to her, which he did, playing simple old melodies that he fancied she must have heard in her youth—I found this gesture of his very charming.

"Then one evening Tino rowed over to Como to visit friends at the Lake Hotel. Matteo did not go, I cannot now remember why, and that evening Tino met Fiora Casani—I never quite understood how it happened.

"Fiora was not like any other woman; I knew her well at one time in Paris. She was, I suppose, an adventuress, but she never behaved in the least like one; she behaved like a trustful and rather spoilt child, which was unexpected and therefore disarming. She was not more than twenty-seven at this time, but already she had had a succession of lovers, one of whom had died leaving her fabulously rich. After that she had married some Hungarian fellow—I think he was the leader of a gipsy band—and when Valentino met her she had just divorced him.

"She was small and one of those supple kind of women who give the impression of being boneless —her hand would seem to melt into yours. She was ugly . . . at least I suppose she was ugly . . . but most men considered her beautiful; Fiora managed, somehow, to create this illusion. Two good points I will admit that she had: her eyes were splendid; luminous, large and intensely appealing— their colour was hazel; and her hair was the perfect Venetian auburn, growing low on the forehead and naturally wavy. Her family came from Venice, I believe, though Fiora herself never spoke about them.

"Well, my friend, from the moment that those

two met there was never any question about what must happen. Each kindled the other and the fire blazed up, so that she who had hitherto subjugated, was herself subjugated because of a passion far more searing than any that had gone before; while Valentino, who was three years her junior, inexperienced, chaste, yet for all that a man, and a man with Roman blood in his veins, Valentino gave her desire for desire with a strength that until then had been lying dormant. And before that fateful evening was passed they had managed to convey these things with their eyes; and Tino went again to Como the next day and the next and the next, and he went alone—having, it seemed, confided in Matteo.

"He took Matteo and me to see her—she was staying on at the Lake Hotel. As always she was very beautifully dressed, if, as always, just a trifle strangely. At this time she was dressing entirely in white; white from head to foot, no suspicion of colour even in her jewels, which were diamonds and pearls. It made her Venetian hair more resplendent and intensified the green of her flecked hazel eyes. Ah, yes, she was cunning over her clothes and rightly—a woman should either go naked or else dress in order to be undressed. I have lived to condemn the Casani for much, but for beautiful clothes I condemn no woman.

"I shall never forget that first visit of ours or the way those two sat and gazed at each other. They were quite unselfconscious and thus unashamed; yet from time to time Tino would tear his eyes from her in order that they might rest on Matteo. But when this happened I could see that she winced, and then she would contrive to do some small thing or to say some small thing that reclaimed his attention. Once she and Matteo exchanged a long look and I saw that each had unsheathed a sword. I felt afraid, yes, actually afraid as one feels at the first sharp clash of weapons.

"We kept it all a secret from the old Marchesa for so long as we remained at Bellaggio, and believe me this was no easy task; that we succeeded was thanks to Matteo. It was he who would help Valentino to escape, often going with him as far as Como in order to allay their mother's suspicions; it was he who frequently carried Tino's letters and flowers to Fiora and brought back her replies; it was he who overhearing his boatman spreading gossip threatened to thrash the fellow until he would never again hold an oar; it was he who was constantly vigilant and on the alert to circumvent scandal.

"I used to watch Matteo with interest not un-mingled with a certain anxiety and pity. So faithful he was, like a faithful dog, and yet so profoundly, so bitterly resentful—I could feel this resentment though he struggled to hide it. But for Tino's sake he continued to serve, continued to guard the perilous secret. All the same there were now occasional quarrels between those two men who had never quarrelled. I stumbled upon a quarrel one day when they thought that they were alone in the garden.

"Tino was saying: 'You *must* love her, I tell you, otherwise it is intolerable—loving you as I do!'

"And Matteo answered hotly: 'Love her? Ah, no! About that you need not deceive yourself, Tino.'

"Then Tino cried out like a petulant child: 'But I want you both; I will have you both; I must and will have you both, Matteo!'

"And it seemed that Tino did want them both, but especially Matteo, according to Fiora. After we had all returned to Rome she sent for me and poured out her grievance: 'Can he come here and be contented for a moment, really contented, Giulio? He cannot. He must always be thinking of that brother of his, of some stupid appointment he has made with Matteo.' She mimicked Tino:

'Mio fratello has asked me to look at his new chestnut hunter.' 'I am going to Frascati with mio fratello this afternoon—I must not be late.' 'I have promised to go with mio fratellino to the tailor; he is having a new uniform fitted.' 'Dio!' she exclaimed, 'it is sickening, preposterous.' And suddenly she began to weep, drying her eyes on my handkerchief as though she were only six years old. I did what I could to make her see reason.

*   *   *   *   *

"Matteo said little but still he guarded, never very far away from his brother. He helped him in all save the most vital thing—not for a moment did he cease to love him. Could he have done so it might have been better, yet who knows—the tie that existed was so strong . . . Meanwhile Tino persisted in wanting them both; the one with passion, the other with a love in whose purity lay its terrific strength. He would often come and see me in my apartment—it was curious how I was constantly forced to take a hand in this now open warfare.

"He would say: 'She is the first, the first woman, Giulio—never can I hope to stop loving Fiora; but then neither can I hope to stop loving him, and I feel that she constantly comes between us.

I am always unhappy when we are together, for when I am with her I think of Matteo; yet when I am with him I think of her. Be patient with me if this sounds like madness . . .' And one evening he cried out: 'Giulio, what must we do, we three who are in hell?' I could find no answer.

"It was now that an added trouble arose: the Marchesa discovered her son's liaison and rather a terrible scene ensued—terrible because of her unnatural coldness. Tino told me that she never once raised her voice, that her words burned like ice. She had heard many things about Fiora's all too conspicuous past, and these she quietly but ruthlessly repeated. Matteo was wonderful, I believe; he reasoned with Tino, he reasoned with their mother, he even tried to reason with Fiora. I heard afterwards that Fiora struck him in the face, but this insult he carefully hid from Tino.

"Then one day Tino announced that he was married. He and Fiora had gone off to Switzerland, where it seemed that he owned some property—I do not understand how the marriage was contrived, but apparently it was perfectly legal. Of course this finished things with his mother; Tino had defied a strict law of the Church. As Fiora's first husband was still alive, the Marchesa did not consider them married, and for Tino to insist that they were made it worse. She ordered her son to leave the house, refusing to receive him again—compromise was anathema to the Marchesa.

"With the closing of the door of the Palazzo della Valda, every Black door in Rome was closed on the couple, and a number of other doors as well. Their so-called marriage was not looked upon kindly; it was one thing to keep a mistress, people said, and quite another to present her as a wife. But Tino was beginning to write his opera and appeared indifferent to public opinion. As for Fiora, she was legally bound to him now, he could not escape, and this seemed to content her.

"Amazing it was to see that spoilt child, that creature of violent moods and caprices, settle down to domesticity; I had never supposed her capable of it. And yet in her own exotic way Fiora had become intensely domestic. She and Tino lived in an atmosphere of white bear-skin rugs, white velvet-pile carpets, tuberoses and other oppressive flowers. Their palazzo was habitually over-heated, for Fiora suffered much from the cold—I often wondered how Tino could stand it. Above all I wondered how Matteo could stand it, he who loved the rarefied air of the mountains, he who so much delighted in climbing great heights—as did Valentino himself, for that matter. But Matteo did stand it; he was nearly always with them whenever he managed to get off duty.

"At that time I myself was frequently there, and I saw some very curious scenes; triangular scenes, when Tino would play while the other two sat near the piano and watched him. Watched him, yes, but they also watched each other, covertly, slyly, under their lashes; not with love—do not think they were falling in love—love was not in their eyes but a thinly veiled hatred. When Tino was present they were outwardly courteous, but their courtesy could never deceive me. I knew them for what they were in their hearts—barbarians grown jealous to the point of madness.

"And indeed Matteo had cause to be jealous. He was like a watch-dog with no one to guard; Fiora had taken his master from him. It was she who now constantly guarded Tino, who kept the place quiet when he was at work, who answered his letters, sorted his bills, and was careful to order food that would tempt him. Sometimes she would even cook for him herself, delighted, it seemed, by such menial tasks. In all things but one she was humbly submissive, but that one she opposed relentlessly; with every feminine wile she possessed she strove to loosen the tie with Matteo. No good. I knew that she would not succeed and I think that Matteo knew this also.

"Sometimes I found Tino and Fiora alone, and I fancied that at moments they were almost happy. Perhaps he would be playing while she turned the score of the opera that he hoped would be world-famous. But if Matteo should chance to come in, then Tino would ask him to turn the pages, thrusting Fiora gently away. And again, he would ask Matteo's advice on all sorts of small matters, his clothes, for instance; and Fiora might shrug her shoulders and smile, but in less controlled moods she would be far from smiling. I was there on the occasion of Tino's new socks, and I heard the astounding quarrel that followed.

"Fiora said: 'I chose those socks for you, Tino. Is that not enough? I consider it should be!'

"And he answered: 'No, amore, it is not. I want Matteo to see the colour; I think he may consider it too bright.'

"Then without the least warning Fiora's self-control broke, and turning she upbraided Matteo: 'You, always you, always you!' she screamed, wringing her hands. 'Dio, how I hate you!'

"Valentino went as white as a sheet. 'Do not say such a terrible thing . . .' he babbled.

"But Matteo's quiet, hard voice broke in: 'She cannot hate me as I hate her, because I hate with the strength of a man, whereas she has only the strength of a woman.'

"Valentino covered his face and wept; he seemed utterly helpless and utterly undone. They went to him and each laid a hand on his arm, as though to console for the wounds they inflicted. Then Fiora said, speaking very softly:

"'I want you to promise us something, my Tino.'

"He looked up. I can see his troubled eyes now. 'You want me to promise you something, Fiora?'

"She nodded. 'You may think it a little strange, for it will not concern you until after your death.'

"At those words I turned rather cold, I admit. Not that I believe in a life after death, it was the tone in which Fiora spoke. . . . There she stood very small, very pale, very calm—her calmness was uncanny after the storm—and she went on speaking in that soft, careful voice which while it caressed was yet terribly insistent.

"She said: 'If you should die before me and Matteo, then I think you will be able to look into our hearts, will be able to judge which of us loves you best. And if you can—if it is possible, Tino— I demand that you will give us a sign, will reveal to us which of the two you have chosen as being the one who is worthier of you. It shall not matter which receives your message, for whichever receives it will tell the other; that is a pact we will make here and now. Matteo and I would keep close together—oh, but very close—if we should lose you, Tino.' She turned to Matteo, whose face had gone grey: 'Is not that so, Matteo?' she asked him.

"I could see that his voice came with difficulty, but he muttered: 'Yes, Fiora—that is so.'

"After this they both looked gravely at Tino as though they expected him to speak; and Tino, in his turn, looked gravely back, and he said: 'God willing, I promise.'

"I felt angry, I did not know what to do, the whole thing struck me as being indecent. Picture it, a ridiculous scene about socks to end with such a preposterous suggestion! As soon as I could I took my leave. Matteo left with me, but once outside I luckily managed to shake him off by pretending that I had an urgent engagement.

*　　　*　　　*　　　*　　　*

"The spring was very wonderful that year, the kind of spring that comes only to Rome. I had been intending to go back to Naples, but Rome held me fast by sheer love of her beauty. In such weather anger and jealousy and hatred seemed as much out of place as drops of crude poison injected into the heart of a rose; I could not help thinking of Matteo and Fiora, and wondering if they were feeling this also.

"I had not seen any of the three for some weeks when one evening I happened to come across Tino. He was leaning on the stone balustrade of the Pincio, staring at the domes and roofs of the city. The moment was perfect beyond belief; a faint golden haze was shrouding St. Peter's, while above the dome the sky was still bright. And out of the mist came the sound of bells, those eternal and challenging bells of Rome that I sometimes believe have saved Christendom . . . this is only the merest fancy of course, but then Rome has the magic that breeds such fancies.

"Tino turned and came forward with outstretched hand. 'You, Giulio, I am so glad to see you,' he said, and his voice sounded glad.

"Then I noticed his expression—it was restless and intensely alive. I had not seen that look on his face for some time, not in fact since his marriage to Fiora.

" 'What weather!' I exclaimed. A banal remark, but remembering the scene I had witnessed, I felt awkward.

"Tino flung out his arms and the gesture seemed full of a kind of anxious, yearning impatience. 'Weather to be going up,' he replied, 'not weather to be suffocating down there in Rome.'

"I knew what he meant; it was the urge to climb, that craving for heights which he shared with Matteo. It was in their blood that craving for heights; they had made a good many fine ascents before Tino's marriage, and always together.

" 'I cannot breathe any more,' he complained. 'I cannot breathe any more down there!'

"A week later I heard that he and Matteo had suddenly decided to go climbing again as soon as the condition of the snow permitted. But they never went; from Matteo I learned that Fiora refused to be left alone, yet would not accompany them to the village which they had intended to make their headquarters.

" 'I have therefore abandoned the idea,' he told me, 'for of course I will not go without Tino. If he lives in a cage then I must share it until he can force the door and escape.'

"This seemed to me very exaggerated and I said so, but he quickly changed the subject.

"Then one day a friend took Matteo for a flight over Rome in a military aeroplane. From that moment he went quite mad about flying and Tino immediately followed suit—I suppose the great altitude was the attraction. I know that Fiora tried to stop Tino, but this time her efforts were unsuccessful. He would leave her and go to the aerodrome where, whenever possible, Matteo would join him—I have heard that they both became excellent pilots. Tino urged Fiora to go up with them, but this she always refused to do, for now she had grown to detest the air. She told me that the air was taking him from her, that he loved her less because of his new craze, and many other foolish things she said, working herself into storms of anger. Nor did Tino make the least effort to be tactful; he would come in and throw open all the windows.

" 'Ma, Dio santo,' I once heard him say, 'this room is intolerable, Fiora—a hot-house. I cannot endure the heat of your rooms!'

"Her eyes filled with tears and I read her thoughts, but that time she controlled herself, saying nothing.

"Then Tino crashed. He had gone up alone so that none of us knew what caused the disaster. All we knew was that his plane nose-dived on the Campagna and that he was practically broken to pieces. He was not killed outright; they got him home and Fiora telephoned at once for me. I went

224

to her, of course, although I could do nothing.

"They had laid Valentino on the long dining-table, and when I arrived I found him still conscious. The Marchesa was there with two strange men: one was a priest, the other a doctor picked up near the place of the accident—I thought that the room smelt of death already. Either side of the table stood Matteo and Fiora, each was holding one of Valentino's hands. Neither of them wept, they seemed perfectly calm. But their eyes . . . the expression I saw in their eyes . . . I cannot describe what I saw in their eyes, perhaps because there are no words that describe it. Tino was appallingly disfigured; there was grass in his face . . . appallingly disfigured . . . Yet strangely enough he was able to speak.

"He said: 'Matteo.' And with more effort: 'Fiora.'

"Fiora stooped and she kissed his bleeding mouth. 'Your promise——' I heard her whisper, 'your promise.'

"He stared at her a moment, then he answered quite loudly: 'Yes—I shall keep it, Fiora.'

*　　　*　　　*　　　*　　　*

"After Tino's death I was called away. My villa at Posilippo needed repairs and I did not go back to Rome for six months. Imagine my amazement when I found on my return that Matteo was sharing Fiora's palazzo. This new scandal was naturally on everyone's lips; all Rome was outraged as, indeed, I was myself until I saw the extraordinary pair—after that I was no longer outraged but frightened.

"I called one afternoon about tea-time and found Fiora alone. She was still wearing white and her face matched her clothes; she was deathly pale—much less like a creature of flesh and blood than the form of that creature carved in marble. She received me kindly but her manner was distant, as though I had been the merest acquaintance, and when she looked at me I could not help feeling that her eyes scarcely registered what they saw. She gave me the impression of a woman whose mind was possessed by some dominating idea that completely excluded all lesser interests. She sat very still, but I knew that she was restless, for she kept glancing up at a clock on the wall. It was one of those costly but maddening clocks that chime the quarters as well as the hours; I can still hear that damnable toy of hers chiming. She talked about trifles and I followed her lead, not daring to assume the rôle of an old friend and question her as I was longing to do—she was gentle yet curiously forbidding.

"I must have been there about an hour when the front door banged and I saw Fiora stiffen. Someone was coming along the hall, someone whose tread was dragging and lifeless. I did not recognise that lifeless tread; I judged it to belong to a person who was old. The next minute Matteo was standing before me.

"We shook hands. 'So you are back, Giulio,' he said dully.

"I nodded. I swear that I could not speak at that moment—it was the change in Matteo.

"He had been such a gallant upstanding fellow, and his face had been so honest, so open; but now he appeared to have shrunk into himself, and his face was not open any more, it was closed, very carefully closed and locked like a book that contains a secret; yet in spite of this—perhaps because I had known him from his childhood—I seemed to be reading in that locked book, and what I read there was dark and unlovely, though I could not give it an actual name, and this scared me, for I hate the intangible, there is always something disconcerting about it.

"Fiora glanced at him sharply. She said: 'Where have you been?'

"And he answered in a flat, mechanical voice:

'I have been to St. Peter's to pray for Tino.'
It was like a child repeating a lesson. Then
he walked across to where Fiora was sitting
and stood by her chair looking at her in silence.

"She smiled, and that smile was intentionally
cruel. 'I prayed for him all night as well as this
morning—all through the night I prayed for my
husband.'

" 'I could not keep awake all night . . .' he
muttered, 'but I asked that more masses should be
said for his soul.' Matteo's voice rose on a note
of aggression. 'For twelve more masses I have
asked!' he said loudly.

" 'I saw to that three days ago,' she replied.
'You are rather late, are you not, Matteo?'

"I sat there like the fool that I felt. Then a
horrible idea came into my head: was this some
gruesome game they were playing? It really did
suggest a game just at first; I almost expected to
hear her call: 'Check-mate!' And they watched
each other—but how they watched. Even when
at last they turned to me I could feel them still
watching, if not with their eyes then with their
hands—their very hands seemed to watch—their
whole bodies seemed on the alert to watch and
thereby to gain some crafty advantage. They had
used to watch during poor Tino's lifetime but not

228

like this, not in the least like this. Since his death the thing had grown monstrously, I felt now that it had become an obsession.

"After a time they recollected themselves and tried, more or less, to entertain me; but their efforts were for ever breaking down. They would ask or answer some trivial question, then start to drift together again. I could almost hear her mind groping for his and his for hers, edging closer by inches; implacable, cunning, but in the dark—foes who must come to grips in the dark. It was pretty horrible, I assure you. Never once did they speak to me directly of Tino, though at last I tried his name as a charm that might exorcise this thing they had raised. But it failed; the moment I mentioned that name I could see that they both became even more watchful. You may never have seen a duel to the death, I have, and I tell you it was like that: thrust, guard; thrust, guard—till the rapier gets home; only, in their case, the duel seemed endless. Matteo was less skilled and less cautious than she was; with my heart in my mouth I would hear him blunder. Yes, my friend, I will say with my heart in my mouth, for this curious combat of minds was exciting. I found myself sickened and excited by turns; repelled and yet gripped in spite of my repulsion. Matteo would blunder over what must have seemed to the uninitiated mere trifles; little everyday tasks that a person might do for someone he loved and not think twice about it. Thus when Fiora mentioned poor Tino's clothes . . .

" 'Matteo,' she said, 'I have pressed Tino's clothes and laid them in the cassone in my room with sprigs of rosemary and lavender.'

"Simple, you will say; just a natural act of affectionate courtesy to the dead. Why should she not press and care for his clothes? Simple, maybe, if one had not divined her intention.

"Matteo sighed heavily—an animal's sigh— horses and dogs sometimes sigh like that, and large jungle beasts when we keep them in prison. He sighed and I knew he would make a slip. He did.

" 'There is all his music,' he murmured, 'it is torn—I noticed that much of it is torn . . .'

"I was watching Fiora and I saw her face change. 'Ma, chè!' she shrugged, with apparent indifference. But I knew that Matteo had lowered his guard and I fancied that, too late, he also perceived this, for he suddenly frowned and bit his lip.

"As for myself, I was being hypnotised by that wholly detestable competition. How else explain my anxiety on behalf of the stupid, incautious Matteo? I heard myself say: 'If the music is torn, then why, in God's name, not mend it at once?'

"He glanced at me with suspicion, I thought, but he went to a bureau and found some gummed-tape, after which he began to repair the music.

"All the time that I was with them he never sat down, whereas Fiora never moved from her seat. When I got up to go she gave me her hand—it was cold, icy cold, like the hand of a dead thing.

"I was hurrying through the hall, when I noticed Tino's portrait with a large bunch of roses beside it. The roses had not been there when I arrived, and I paused to examine a black-edged card propped conspicuously against their foliage. The card bore this inscription: 'To Tino the beloved from his brother, in token of their devotion.' As I read someone came up quietly behind me and I turned to see Fiora staring over my shoulder—her face was literally distorted by rage. Without more ado I fled from the place, thankful when I found myself in the sunshine.

*   *   *   *   *

"That evening Matteo paid me a visit. He sank down heavily in my armchair like a man who was weary unto death. After a minute he said: 'Listen, Giulio, you have known me ever since I was a child; do you consider that I am truthful?'

"I answered at once: 'But I know you are; I know that you have always been truthful.'

"Then he said: 'I am living in Fiora's house. Why do you suppose I am living there? Do you think as the others think . . . basely, vilely?'

" 'No, no!' I exclaimed, 'I swear I do not.'

" 'Very well, then, Giulio,' he went on, 'I will tell you. We must live together, Fiora and I; it is part of the pact—you heard us make it. She and I agreed not to leave each other if Tino died, until he gave us a sign. He will give it because he never broke a promise. Fiora believes this, we both believe it, and while we are waiting we try to serve him—each in our separate ways we try to serve. But—and this is very important, Giulio—we have sworn to tell each other all we do, even down to the most trivial acts of service. Not beforehand, ah, no, that would be unfair . . . very unfair, would it not, my Giulio? We each keep the right to prove our devotion to Tino independently of the other. Fiora thinks. I think. We rack our brains as to what will impress him—we are always at it. It is hard because she is much cleverer than I am; it is really amazing how clever she is, the subtle and ingratiating things she thinks of. And so quick, she frequently thinks of things first—those extra masses, she thought of them first.

Sometimes I feel that I must crush her with my hands—she is really too small to be so ingenious. It would not take a minute to crush her with my hands . . .'

"I stared at him aghast. 'And you imagine that Tino is made happy by this devilish pact?' I stammered.

" 'That I do not know,' he replied. 'I know only that we three are bound together until something that I cannot yet envisage is lived through—sloughed off, flung away and done with for ever.'

"He paused and I lunged with intent to wound: 'But Tino loved Fiora, whereas you hate her.'

"Matteo nodded. 'You are right, I hate her.' Then he sprang to his feet. 'Tino was my brother, my own flesh and blood; he was part of my body, he is part of my soul—that is why I hate her. What has this woman to do with us?'

"I retorted, trying hard to collect myself: 'Quite soon you and Fiora will both be insane. Never have I heard anything so outrageous, so degrading to the memory of the dead.'

"I saw at once that I had failed of my mark, for he answered: 'It is natural you should feel like this. I can never hope to make you understand; therefore, my friend, let us not discuss it. What is the use?' And with that he left me.

*　　　　*　　　　*　　　　*　　　　*

"The next thing that happened was not unexpected: Matteo was forced to leave his regiment. I felt sorry for he might have had such a fine career, but of course I had known all along that it must come; people had been spreading the wildest rumours.

"Then about four months after I had last seen him I heard that he and Fiora had left Rome. I had purposely kept away from them both, but now I went straight to Fiora's palazzo in order to ask for Matteo's address. I found the place completely deserted, and concluded that they had decided to fly from the scandal they themselves had created.

"I tried to put them out of my mind, but I could not; from that moment they started to haunt me. Talk of the dead, the dead were not in it with those two when it came to a matter of haunting! Wherever I went, whatever I did, I was always being reminded of them. Sometimes at night I would lie wide awake, struggling to reduce the whole affair to the sane and comfortable limits of reason. For two years they were never far from my thoughts, so that when the Marchesa sent for me one day rather suddenly I felt no surprise at learning that she wished to talk of Matteo.

"I found her sitting very stern and composed

in the hard straight-backed chair she always affected. With her usual abruptness she came to the point; I was taken aback at what she demanded, though I should not have been—I, who knew the Marchesa.

"She said: 'Santaspina, go and find my son. I need him because I am now nearly ninety. Therefore I wish you to bring him to Rome and at once, if you please.'

"This seemed a large order, but I nodded, for her proud old eyes were upon me. Then again, I had known her all my life and my father and mother had known her before me. I remembered that Matteo was the last of his house, an honourable and courageous house that had sacrificed much for the sake of the Faith. Not that I approve of the Church, I do not; still, true courage is fine for whatever cause.

"Getting up, I bowed over her hand and kissed it. 'Surely I will do my best,' I told her.

"She thanked me with that arrogant manner of hers—it was rather as an empress might have thanked a slave. After which I perceived that I was dismissed. Ah, well, the Marchesa was a splendid survival.

*　　　*　　　*　　　*　　　*

"I had undertaken a difficult task, more difficult than I had anticipated. Professional aid I dared not employ, the Marchesa would never have forgiven such a thing; she expected me to fill the rôle of detective. I should hardly have believed it possible that people could evade pursuit so completely. I kept getting clues and losing them again; once I traced the couple to London, then to Cornwall, but I always seemed to arrive too late—they would just have gone, leaving no address behind them. For eight months I wandered about over Europe, having failed to obtain any information that led me to think they were farther afield, and I hoped that I had caught them at last in Budapest, but once again I was just too late, they had left for the Upper Tatra. However, this time their address was known for some reason, and not even waiting for a meal I rushed out of the hotel and continued the pursuit, so afraid was I that they might escape me.

"I am not going to weary you with the details of my journey through that wild, God-forsaken country. It was made for the most part in a ramshackle carriage behind half-broken Hungarian horses. At last I arrived at a straggling village high up in the Carpathians; a primitive place miles from anything—a most melancholy place, neglected, desolate and forgotten.

"I was pretty well spent, but I meant to get it over, and I hurried straight up to Matteo's bedroom at the dirty, poverty-stricken inn. I flung open the door without even knocking. Matteo was standing with his back to the door; he was gazing intently out of the window, I suppose at the mountains that were flushed by sunset. I cannot remember precisely what I said, but as he turned round I grasped his hand as if I would never again let it go. Then I think we sat down . . . Yes, of course we sat down, and I told Matteo my reason for coming. He was calm, I thought, to the verge of aloofness; not unwelcoming in his manner towards me . . . it was rather as though he were not really there, as though nothing that I could do or say would recall him from some immeasurable distance. And gentle, my God, he had grown so gentle; I could feel this when he tried to force his attention, tried to drag himself back. . . . A great courtesy appeared to envelop the man like a mantle; it appeared to envelop him fold upon fold, and somehow it made me feel ill at ease—I was conscious of having coarsened in fibre. And his eyes were very clear, very young. His face also was younger than I had ever seen it, younger than it had been when he was a child,

because now there was something indestructible
about it; and yet it was terribly lined and worn.
. . . It looked like a meadow ravaged by war;
I have known pasturelands at the Front like
that, with all sorts of little new flowering things
springing up and up to cover the scars as though
life were the only reality . . .

"I said: 'But you will return to us, Matteo?'

"And he answered: 'No, we cannot return. We
two must wait here for the sign from Tino.'

"My friend, I wanted to think him mad, but I
could not, and this I shall always find strange. He
explained very little, but I understood that his
presence there was due to the mountains, that in
some way he connected them with the pact. He
did not seem able to put this into words, did not
seem very clear about it, I thought, but I felt that
his mind was dwelling on great heights, that the
spell of the mountains lay heavy upon him. I
forced myself to fulfil my duty, which was obviously to leave no stone unturned to take Matteo
home to his mother. But when I spoke of the
Marchesa's great age he appeared to think old age
a happy thing.

"'She will not miss me for long,' he said; 'it
is happy to be near the end of the journey.'

"I tried yet again and now I tried Fiora, believing that the mention of her might rouse him. 'This is a desolate sort of place, I cannot think how Fiora stands it,' I ventured. And, greatly daring, I ventured yet more. 'If you still wish to keep Fiora chained to your side, I advise you to take her away at once, otherwise you may discover that she has escaped you!'

"But he only smiled. 'That would not hurt us—not now—because we have learned to trust each other. What can it matter which one of us is chosen so long as Tino finds peace and contentment?'

"Then, God forgive me, I did a vile thing. In my will to drive this man back to the world, to tear him away from I knew not what, to drag his mind down so that I could grasp it and hold it and perhaps make it serve my purpose, I used the unholy spur of his past—once more I accused Matteo of hating. 'Peace,' I cried, 'is it you who talk about peace when you know in your heart how you hate the woman!'

"He stared as though scarcely understanding my words. 'How can I hate what Tino loves—I who love Tino?' And his voice was bewildered. After this he seemed disinclined to speak any more, so we sat on together in silence.

*　　　*　　　*　　　*　　　*

"I did not see Fiora until supper that evening and she struck me as having changed very little. I detected the old sharp antagonism in her eyes whenever she looked at Matteo, and when Tino was mentioned her voice became hard, hard and possessive—it was all there still: the anger, the mistrust, the bitterness. But Matteo's face remained calm and withdrawn; he must have been living in some kind of dream if he thought that Fiora had really changed .... or was it perhaps the change in himself that had made him wish to perceive only goodness? I do not pretend to know what it was, but I do know that he seemed to have outlived resentment.

"I was finding the whole thing intolerably painful, so that when Matteo left us after supper I turned upon Fiora furiously. 'Are you madder than ever, you two?' I demanded. 'I have come to take Matteo back to Rome, and be careful that you do not attempt to stop me!'

" 'Do you think I enjoy being here?' she retorted. 'This is Matteo's doing, not mine. Of course it is a trick, some abominable trick.'

" 'Oh, for God's sake leave him and end it!' I stormed, feeling thoroughly unnerved by the situation.

"Fiora frowned. 'No, my Giulio, I will certainly

not leave him. He thinks that Tino is now very near us and this may well be. But I read Matteo's thoughts; they are cruel, he is trying to drive me to despair in these horrible mountains; he desires me to go so that he may be left alone with Tino.'

" 'Heaven pity you,' I said, and indeed I meant it.

*　　*　　*　　*　　*

"Well, I stayed on hoping to persuade Matteo to return, but I found that argument was fruitless. Moreover, Fiora was my enemy, cleverly circumventing all my efforts to get Matteo to myself for a moment—I suppose she feared that once back in Rome she might be unable to keep him with her. It was terrible sometimes, I marvel that I stood it, she so bitter and he so unresentful; she believing the worst, he believing the best—and always that unearthly courtesy of his which nothing could disturb, not even Fiora. But for his mother I must have thrown it up—I dreaded to meet the Marchesa empty-handed.

"Then one morning Matteo could not be found; moreover, he had not slept in his bed nor had he been seen about the village. Fiora was much less alarmed than I was; she was used, it seemed, to his lonely excursions. She declared that he frequently went out at night and wandered off by himself into the mountains.

" 'And I dare not follow him,' she complained. 'I grow giddy, so he knows that I dare not follow.'

"I pushed her aside and left the room; at that moment I could not endure her near me.

"I think you have seen the Carpathians, if you have then you must remember their grimness. No snow to soften those terrible peaks—too steep for the snow to cling, I was told—in any case, I never saw the snow, only hard, cruel rock against the skyline. As I looked at those mountains my heart misgave me, and all that day there was no Matteo, and by sundown he had not yet returned.

"I said nothing to Fiora, but I went to his bedroom; some instinct urged me to lock the door and after I had done this to examine his papers. His papers did not help me at first, then I came on a letter that was obviously recent; it had been re-directed from Budapest. I looked at the date on the local postmark and found that it had reached him two days ago; the letter had been written from a place in Cornwall. But I think I will let you read it for yourself; it is in my despatch box. I brought it to England just in case I was able to trace the people, though of course it's fairly old history by now, and so far I have failed to get in touch with them."

Santaspina got up and fetched the letter. I have it before me on my desk as I write; he was willing that I should take a copy. The letter ran as follows:

"DEAR MARCHESE DELLA VALDA,—

"What I am about to say may surprise you in view of our very slight acquaintance—if so I trust that you will forgive me.

"But let me explain the point of this letter: my wife and I have been trying just lately to develop the power of automatic writing, and we seem to remember that when you were in Cornwall you said you were interested in such matters. At all events your name appears in the script which I enclose. It seems risky to send it, especially through the foreign post, but we'd rather you saw the original as a copy would be so much less convincing.

"We both hope that you may be willing to help us in regard to those points that we cannot understand and which, if they mean anything to you, are good evidence for the super-normal.

"You will notice that the word 'Brunnenberg' appears together with the words 'near summit.' Do you know of a place that goes by that name? The words 'near summit' suggest a mountain. There is also a word that we think must be

243

'chapel.' Do you know of any chapel in this connection? My wife and I are completely in the dark and must, therefore, depend upon you for assistance. Then what can the words 'Graue Schwester' mean; and the words 'branch left.' Some sort of directions? The quotation from Isaiah means nothing to us either, nor do we recognise the name 'Tino.'

"You will find several other things in the script that seem to refer directly to yourself. The writing is not very clear I'm afraid, but considering its nature it's not too bad, and I know that you can speak and read English. Please return the script as soon as possible, together with your notes if you are kind enough to make them.

"By the greatest good fortune I heard from Mr. Wallace that you were quite recently in Budapest. He has sent me the name of the hotel where he met you and where he believes you may still be staying. I am sending this letter addressed to you there in the hope that they will forward it if you have left.

"Apologising for troubling you,
"I remain,
"Sincerely yours,
"GEORGE CAMPBELL."

I laid down the letter and looked at Santaspina: "Well?" I said.

He appeared reluctant to speak, then he shrugged his shoulders and went on with his story.

"It all seemed fairly clear to me at the time. There was a mountain called the Brunnenberg and it happened to be quite close to the village. I knew that Matteo had been waiting for a sign, and when I read that letter I never doubted for a moment that he thought the sign had come, I felt certain that he had gone to the mountain believing that he would meet his brother, that Tino would at last reveal his choice, that at last the fearful bondage would be ended.

"I ransacked the room for the automatic writing but could not find it, and so I concluded that Matteo had taken the paper with him. Then I slipped the letter into my pocket and made my way to the village at once—I meant to try part of the ascent that evening and was lucky enough to find a peasant who would guide me.

"They all did what they could to be helpful and kind. Someone lent me a pair of string-soled shoes without which it is impossible to climb in the Carpathians; someone else put together a pack of food, and someone else gave me a rosary—I found them good-hearted, if superstitious.

"But none of them had ever heard of a chapel in the vicinity of the mountain, so I had to rely on my other clue, the Graue Schwester, and this clue proved useful. The Graue Schwester were known —it appeared they were two sharp rocks not far from the summit.

"I am nothing of a climber, and climbing in those parts is always a fairly difficult business, yet I managed somehow to begin the ascent, though I never expected to get back alive, for at first we had only a full moon to work by, and what glimmers we could extract from our lanterns. We spent the best part of that night in a hut, keeping ourselves warm as well as we could, and just before daybreak we set out again and finally reached the Graue Schwester. But here my guide and I had a dispute, for I wished to abide by the words in the letter, and the words in the letter said: 'branch left.' On the other hand, he wished to keep straight ahead, protesting that it was the only known track; I argued for more than half-an-hour with him. In the end I resorted to bribery and he consented to try my way, though not without the greatest reluctance. And a terrifying climb it turned out to be. I hope I shall never be asked to repeat it, though after a bit it grew easier, for the ledge we were following widened a little. Then, quite suddenly, we had rounded a crag and were staring at a plateau-like piece of ground upon which had been built a tiny chapel.

"It was all in ruins, a mere shell of a place, roofless, and with only its four walls standing; but a stone crucifix very old and defaced was still above what had once been the entrance. My guide stopped abruptly and crossed himself; he was shaking with terror. They are so superstitious that he probably thought the whole thing a vision.

"I left him and hurried across to the chapel. . . . When I got there I had not far to seek. . . . Matteo lay dead just inside the doorway, and from the position of his body I thought that death must have come to him while he was kneeling—he was lying crumpled up, his knees were bent and his strong, shapely hands were clasped together. There was something in his hands: a piece of paper with minute, rather queer-looking writing upon it. His face was composed, neither happy nor un-happy. It struck me as being an empty face . . . it seemed completely empty of Matteo.

"I stood there looking down at this man whom I had known since the days of his childhood, and suddenly I was filled with deep joy. . . . I do not know where that joy can have come from, I only know that I wanted to shout—that I wanted to shout in the presence of death as the young will shout for the splendour of living. Stooping, I tried to release the paper; I could not because his hands had stiffened, but I managed to make out a few scattered words: 'Brunnenberg,' and then something that looked like 'come.' Then a scrawl that I fancied was meant for 'dawn.' Then—and this was quite clearly written—'Matteo.' Finally I tore off the end of the script in order that I might examine it better. Sitting on the ground I spread it on my knee and smoothed away the creases as best I could. . . . At that moment the sun blazed out over the ruin, over Matteo and the paper I held. I bent closer and these were the words I read:

" 'How beautiful upon the mountains are the feet of him that bringeth good tidings, that publisheth peace.' "

Printed in July 2019
by Rotomail Italia S.p.A., Vignate (MI) - Italy